DISCARDED
BY
MEMPHIS PUBLIC LIBRARY

Generously Donated by the

MEMPHIS LIBRARY FOUNDATION

Immigration to North America

Cuban Immigrants

Pete Spranger

Asylum Seekers

Central American Immigrants

Chinese Immigrants

Cuban Immigrants

Indian Immigrants

Mexican Immigrants

Middle Eastern Immigrants

Refugees

Rights & Responsibilities of Citizenship

South American Immigrants

Undocumented Immigration and Homeland Security

Immigration to North America

Cuban Immigrants

Pete Spranger

Senior Consulting Editor Stuart Anderson
former Associate Commissioner for Policy and Planning,
U.S. Citizenship and Immigration Services

Introduction by Marian L. Smith, Historian,
U.S. Citizenship and Immigration Services

Introduction by Peter A. Hammerschmidt,
former First Secretary, Permanent Mission of Canada to the United Nations

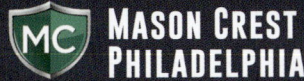

Mason Crest
450 Parkway Drive, Suite D
Broomall, PA 19008
www.masoncrest.com

©2017 by Mason Crest, an imprint of National Highlights, Inc.

All rights reserved. No part of this publication may be reproduced or transmitted in any form or by any means, electronic or mechanical, including photocopying, recording, taping, or any information storage and retrieval system, without permission from the publisher.

Printed and bound in the United States of America.

CPSIA Compliance Information: Batch #INA2016.
For further information, contact Mason Crest at 1-866-MCP-Book.

First printing
1 3 5 7 9 8 6 4 2

Library of Congress Cataloging-in-Publication Data

on file at the Library of Congress
ISBN: 978-1-4222-3685-7 (hc)
ISBN: 978-1-4222-8102-4 (ebook)

Immigration to North America series ISBN: 978-1-4222-3679-6

Table of Contents

Introduction: The Changing Face of the United States   6
    by Marian L. Smith

Introduction: The Changing Face of Canada   10
    by Peter A. Hammerschmidt

1. **Success and Sadness**   15
2. **Why Cubans Want to Leave**   21
3. **A History of Cuban Migration**   45
4. **New American Lives**   67
5. **Old Traditions Lost and Kept**   79
6. **A Community's Challenges**   89
7. **The Future of Cuban Immigration**   97

Famous Cuban Americans   102
Series Glossary of Key Terms   104
Further Reading   105
Internet Resources   106
Index   107
Contributors   111

KEY ICONS TO LOOK FOR:

Words to Understand: These words with their easy-to-understand definitions will increase the reader's understanding of the text, while building vocabulary skills.

Sidebars: This boxed material within the main text allows readers to build knowledge, gain insights, explore possibilities, and broaden their perspectives by weaving together additional information to provide realistic and holistic perspectives.

Research Projects: Readers are pointed toward areas of further inquiry connected to each chapter. Suggestions are provided for projects that encourage deeper research and analysis.

Text-Dependent Questions: These questions send the reader back to the text for more careful attention to the evidence presented there.

Series Glossary of Key Terms: This back-of-the book glossary contains terminology used throughout this series. Words found here increase the reader's ability to read and comprehend higher-level books and articles in this field.

The Changing Face of the United States

Marian L. Smith, Historian
U.S. Citizenship and Immigration Services

Americans commonly assume that immigration today is very different than immigration of the past. The immigrants themselves appear to be unlike immigrants of earlier eras. Their language, their dress, their food, and their ways seem strange. At times people fear too many of these new immigrants will destroy the America they know. But has anything really changed? Do new immigrants have any different effect on America than old immigrants a century ago? Is the American fear of too much immigration a new development? Do immigrants really change America more than America changes the immigrants? The very subject of immigration raises many questions.

In the United States, immigration is more than a chapter in a history book. It is a continuous thread that links the present moment to the first settlers on North American shores. From the first colonists' arrival until today, immigrants have been met by Americans who both welcomed and feared them. Immigrant contributions were always welcome—on the farm, in the fields, and in the factories. Welcoming the poor, the persecuted, and the "huddled masses" became an American principle. Beginning with the original Pilgrims' flight from religious persecution in the 1600s, through the Irish migration to escape starvation in the 1800s, to the relocation of Central Americans seeking refuge from civil wars in the 1980s and 1990s, the United States has considered itself a haven for the destitute and the oppressed.

But there was also concern that immigrants would not adopt American ways, habits, or language. Too many immigrants might overwhelm America. If so, the dream of the Founding Fathers for United States government and society would be destroyed. For this reason, throughout American history some have argued that limiting or ending immigration is our patriotic duty. Benjamin Franklin feared there were so many German immigrants in Pennsylvania the Colonial Legislature would begin speaking German. "Progressive" leaders of the early 1900s feared that immigrants who could not read and understand the English language were not only exploited by "big business," but also served as the foundation for "machine politics" that undermined the U.S. Constitution. This theme continues today, usually voiced by those who bear no malice toward immigrants but who want to preserve American ideals.

Have immigrants changed? In colonial days, when most colonists were of English descent, they considered Germans, Swiss, and French immigrants as different. They were not "one of us" because they spoke a different language. Generations later, Americans of German or French descent viewed Polish, Italian, and Russian immigrants as strange. They were not "like us" because they had a different religion, or because they did not come from a tradition of constitutional government. Recently, Americans of Polish or Italian descent have seen Nicaraguan, Pakistani, or Vietnamese immigrants as too different to be included. It has long been said of American immigration that the latest ones to arrive usually want to close the door behind them.

It is important to remember that fear of individual immigrant groups seldom lasted, and always lessened. Benjamin Franklin's anxiety over German immigrants disappeared after those immigrants' sons and daughters helped the nation gain independence in the Revolutionary War. The Irish of the mid-1800s were among the most hated immigrants, but today we all wear green on St. Patrick's Day. While a century ago it was feared that Italian and other Catholic immigrants would vote as directed by the Pope, today that controversy is only a vague memory. Unfortunately, some ethnic groups continue their efforts to earn acceptance. The African

Americans' struggle continues, and some Asian Americans, whose families have been in America for generations, are the victims of current anti-immigrant sentiment.

Time changes both immigrants and America. Each wave of new immigrants, with their strange language and habits, eventually grows old and passes away. Their American-born children speak English. The immigrants' grandchildren are completely American. The strange foods of their ancestors—spaghetti, baklava, hummus, or tofu—become common in any American restaurant or grocery store. Much of what the immigrants brought to these shores is lost, principally their language. And what is gained becomes as American as St. Patrick's Day, Hanukkah, or Cinco de Mayo, and we forget that it was once something foreign.

Recent immigrants are all around us. They come from every corner of the earth to join in the American Dream. They will continue to help make the American Dream a reality, just as all the immigrants who came before them have done.

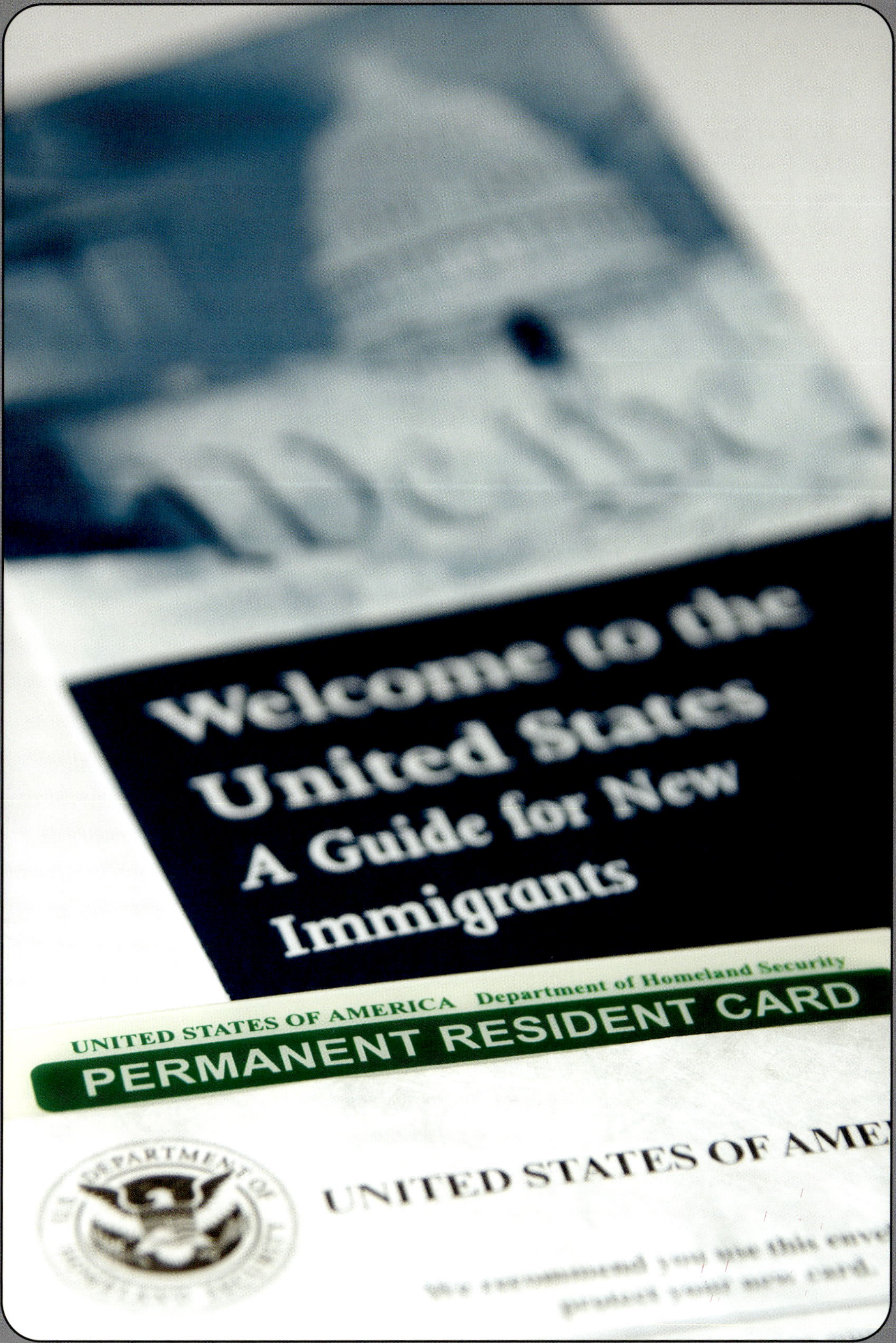
Welcome to the
United States
A Guide for New
Immigrants
UNITED STATES OF AMERICA Department of Homeland Security
PERMANENT RESIDENT CARD
UNITED STATES OF AME

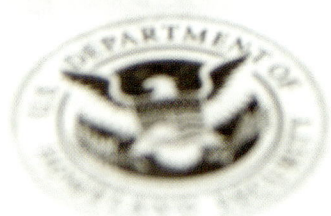

The Changing Face of Canada

Peter A. Hammerschmidt
former First Secretary, Permanent Mission of Canada to the United Nations

Throughout Canada's history, immigration has shaped and defined the very character of Canadian society. The migration of peoples from every part of the world into Canada has profoundly changed the way we look, speak, eat, and live. Through close and distant relatives who left their lands in search of a better life, all Canadians have links to immigrant pasts. We are a nation built by and of immigrants.

Two parallel forces have shaped the history of Canadian immigration. The enormous diversity of Canada's immigrant population is the most obvious. In the beginning came the enterprising settlers of the "New World," the French and English colonists. Soon after came the Scottish, Irish, and Northern and Central European farmers of the 1700s and 1800s. As the country expanded westward during the mid-1800s, migrant workers began arriving from China, Japan, and other Asian countries. And the turbulent twentieth century brought an even greater variety of immigrants to Canada, from the Caribbean, Africa, India, and Southeast Asia.

So while English- and French-Canadians are the largest ethnic groups in the country today, neither group alone represents a majority of the population. A large and vibrant multicultural mix makes up the rest, particularly in Canada's major cities. Toronto, Vancouver, and Montreal alone are home to people from over 200 ethnic groups!

Less obvious but equally important in the evolution of Canadian immigration has been hope. The promise of a better life lured Europeans and

Americans seeking cheap (sometimes even free) farmland. Thousands of Scots and Irish arrived to escape grinding poverty and starvation. Others came for freedom, to escape religious and political persecution. Canada has long been a haven to the world's dispossessed and disenfranchised— Dutch and German farmers cast out for their religious beliefs, black slaves fleeing the United States, and political refugees of despotic regimes in Europe, Africa, Asia, and South America.

The two forces of diversity and hope, so central to Canada's past, also shaped the modern era of Canadian immigration. Following the Second World War, Canada drew heavily on these influences to forge trailblazing immigration initiatives.

The catalyst for change was the adoption of the Canadian Bill of Rights in 1960. Recognizing its growing diversity and Canadians' changing attitudes towards racism, the government passed a federal statute barring discrimination on the grounds of race, national origin, color, religion, or sex. Effectively rejecting the discriminatory elements in Canadian immigration policy, the Bill of Rights forced the introduction of a new policy in 1962. The focus of immigration abruptly switched from national origin to the individual's potential contribution to Canadian society. The door to Canada was now open to every corner of the world.

Welcoming those seeking new hopes in a new land has also been a feature of Canadian immigration in the modern era. The focus on economic immigration has increased along with Canada's steadily growing economy, but political immigration has also been encouraged. Since 1945, Canada has admitted tens of thousands of displaced persons, including Jewish Holocaust survivors, victims of Soviet crackdowns in Hungary and Czechoslovakia, and refugees from political upheaval in Uganda, Chile, and Vietnam.

Prior to 1978, however, these political refugees were admitted as an exception to normal immigration procedures. That year, Canada revamped its refugee policy with a new Immigration Act that explicitly affirmed Canada's commitment to the resettlement of refugees from oppression. Today, the admission of refugees remains a central part of

Canadian immigration law and regulations.

Amendments to economic and political immigration policy have continued, refining further the bold steps taken during the modern era. Together, these initiatives have turned Canada into one of the world's few truly multicultural states.

Unlike the process of assimilation into a "melting pot" of cultures, immigrants to Canada are more likely to retain their cultural identity, beliefs, and practices. This is the source of some of Canada's greatest strengths as a society. And as a truly multicultural nation, diversity is not seen as a threat to Canadian identity. Quite the contrary—diversity is Canadian identity.

1 Success and Sadness

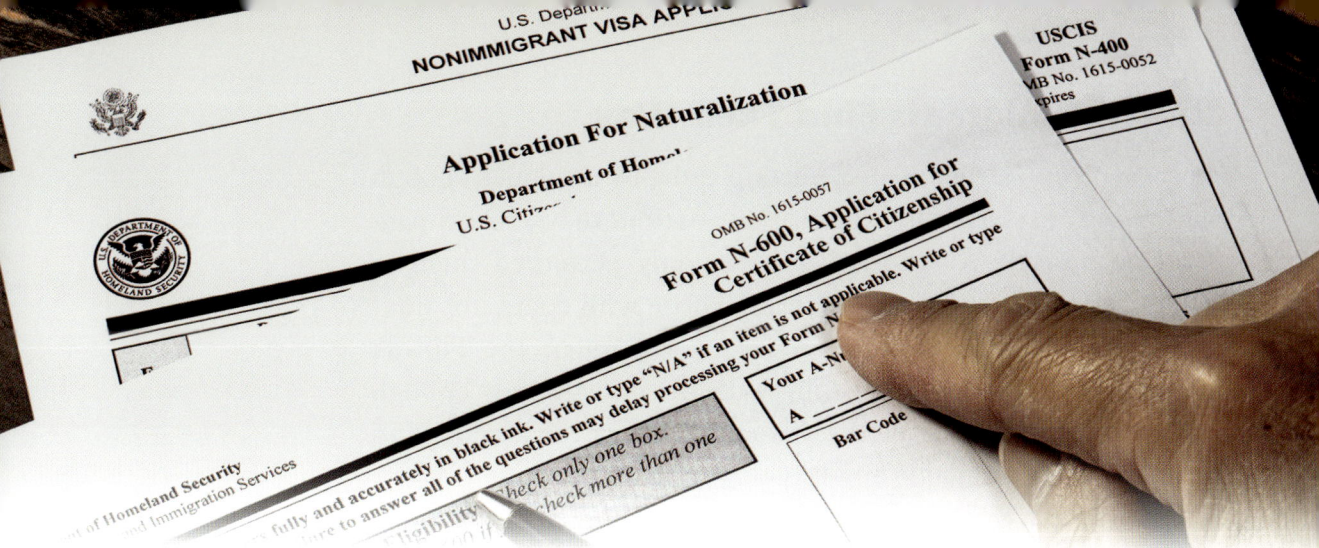

There aren't many groups that have moved toward attaining the "American dream" as rapidly as the Cuban exiles. But there aren't many groups, either, that have a stronger affinity for the homeland they had to leave behind.

The first major exodus from Cuba, an island nation less than 100 miles (161 kilometers) from the Florida Keys, brought exiles to North America during the early 1960s. Nearly everyone came to get away from the regime of Fidel Castro, who took power in 1959. Since then, other Cubans have been seeking freedoms denied them in their native country.

Relatively few Cubans have settled in Canada. The 2011 Canadian census counted 21,440 residents of Cuban ancestry. However, that represented a fourfold increase since the 2001 census. Because of their small numbers, Cubans living in Canada have not made a large impact on Canadian life, although defections of small Cuban groups in 1998 and in 2002 have raised some national awareness of the exiles' situation.

The United States, by contrast, has welcomed large numbers of Cubans. In 2012, according to data from the U.S. Census Bureau, nearly 2 million people of Cuban ancestry were living in the United States. It is in the United States that Cuban exiles and their American-born children have had the strongest impact.

◀ A U.S. Navy ship transports Cuban refugees to the naval base at Guantánamo Bay, Cuba, after they were picked up at sea. Since the early 1960s, large waves of Cuban refugees have left for Canada and the United States seeking freedom. They have traveled by plane, ship, and even makeshift boats and rafts.

Cuban Immigrants Find Their Way

Most members of the first exile group came by airplane. Though they were considered the elite of their nation, they arrived penniless because the Castro government only permitted them to bring a couple of changes of clothes. Those who could not travel by airplane braved the treacherous waters of the Florida Straits in homemade rafts, taking with them just barely enough food and water to survive the voyage. Most of them arrived in Miami, the closest major city to Cuba.

At first, the exiles were unable to practice their professions and had to take whatever low-paying jobs they could find so that their families would have the necessary provisions. Stories abound in the Cuban community about surgeons who cleaned toilets, or professors who worked in small retail shops, earning little more than American teenagers did at a part-time job.

By the end of the 1960s, however, many Cuban immigrants had started their own businesses, and the group's professionals reestablished themselves. As years went on, they were joined by other immigrating Cubans, who had less formal education but were just as eager to succeed.

The first wave of Cuban immigrants did not stray far from its roots, but the majority of the sons and daughters—who had come from Cuba as children or were born in the United States during their parents' years of struggle—grew up bilingual and bicultural. By the 1970s and 1980s, many individuals in this second generation had graduated from college and begun their own

Words to Understand in This Chapter

elite—a small group of people who exercise influence on a country.
exiles—people who leave their nation for political reasons.
exodus—a departure of a large number of people from a place.
socioeconomic—having to do with social and economic factors.

careers. Those with children were parents to a generation that only knew life in America, two whole generations removed from the turbulent period of Castro's rise to power.

Today, severe economic hardship is largely a thing of the past for most Cuban immigrant families. In terms of socioeconomic indicators such as average income, education, and home ownership, Cuban Americans are not very different from the non-Hispanic white population. In other words, even though the post-1959 wave of Cuban immigrants has been in the United States for only a couple of generations, they have quickly reached a level of success comparable to that of American families who have been in the country much longer.

At the national level, Cuban Americans have played a significant role in politics, largely because they are heavily concentrated in Florida, a key state in presidential elections. In the controversial election of 2000, Republican George W. Bush rode a three-to-one advantage among Cuban American voters to a razor-thin victory in the Sunshine State—which in turn enabled him to claim the presidency.

Bush's performance among Florida's Cuban American voters wasn't surprising: for a long time, that constituency overwhelmingly favored the Republican Party. However, the situation is quite different today, with the Republican and Democratic parties now drawing comparable levels of support from the Cuban American community. In fact, the 2012 presidential election saw Democrat Barack Obama outpoll Republican Mitt Romney by about 2 percentage points among Cuban Americans in Florida. This shift in voting patterns is partly attributable to demographic changes. Cubans who left their homeland in the immediate aftermath of Castro's takeover remain solidly Republican, crediting the Republican Party with adopting a harder line against communism in general and the Cuban regime in particular. But their American-born children and grandchildren tend not to care as much about Cuban politics, and most of them gravitate toward the Democratic Party. Nationally, the political influence of Cuban Americans can be expected to decline as they vote less and less as a unified bloc.

At the local level, though, Cubans have left an indelible mark on southern Florida. This is especially true in Miami, a city where speaking Spanish is as common as speaking English, even in the wealthiest neighborhoods and the most prominent executive boardrooms. In Miami, Cuban Americans run businesses large and small, Cuban American artists comprise an important part of the cultural scene, and Cuban American politicians are consistently elected to municipal office, the Florida legislature, and the U.S. Congress.

Remembering the Homeland

Yet for all these forms of success, many Cuban Americans by and large feel a great sadness. Cuban immigrants are grateful that they could resettle during a time of need, and that they

Ethnicity and Race

The major ethnic categories of North Americans are white, black, Asian, Native American, and Hispanic. Since ethnicity and race are often used interchangeably to describe people, it may be confusing to hear that a Hispanic person can also be white, black, Native American, or Asian.

To dispel the confusion, it is important to first recognize that the Hispanic population encompasses a wide range of people. Cubans, for example, are just one group of many referred to as "Hispanic" (many people from Latin American countries or of Latin American descent prefer the term *Latino*). The term *Hispanic* also refers to Argentineans, Mexicans, Puerto Ricans, Nicaraguans, Spaniards, or any people who were born in—or who trace their heritage to—any of the world's 20 Spanish-speaking lands. Hispanics thus include people of every color who share specific historical and cultural attributes, but they do not form a single race.

Like the United States and Canada, most Hispanic countries are made up of people of different races who have close or distant ties to other countries. In Cuba, the largest racial groups are whites and blacks. The majority of white Cubans are the descendants of Spaniards who immigrated to Cuba while it was a Spanish colony or during its first decades as an independent state. But there are also Cubans whose ancestors arrived on the island after leaving Italy, Ireland, England, and even China. Cuba also had a significant Jewish population.

Cuba's other large population is of African ancestry. In the United States and in Cuba, a significant number of black people trace their lineage to enslaved Africans brought to work on the plantations.

found opportunities that allowed them and their children to succeed, yet many still long for the Cuba they had to leave behind.

The sons and daughters of the original exiles assimilated more easily, yet they grew up listening to their parents' stories of loss. Many who have received this mixed heritage struggle with what it means to be an American of Cuban descent, and are thus are faced with pressing questions: How different are we, really, from other Americans? Should our main language be English or Spanish? How committed should we be to bringing democracy to Cuba?

Finally, there are the issues facing the youngest generation, the grandchildren of those who left Cuba as adults, those born in America and who only know life in the United States. Of course, as children they ask more basic questions: Should I learn enough Spanish to speak to my grandparents? Do I want hamburger for dinner, or rice with black beans? But upon closer observation, it seems they ask the same question their parents ask themselves: How Cuban am I, and how American? In the end, Cuban Americans have to answer that question individually. But there is no doubt that their Cuban roots remain with them in some way.

Text-Dependent Questions

1. In what decade did large numbers of Cubans first begin immigrating to the United States? Why?
2. What body of water separates Cuba from Florida?
3. Approximately how many people of Cuban ancestry live in the United States?

Research Project

According to recent data from the U.S. Census Bureau, almost half (48 percent) of all Cuban Americans live in Miami-Dade County, Florida. Using a library or the Internet, find out how Cuban Americans have put their cultural stamp on this region. Pay particular attention to the city of Miami. Organize your findings and write a two-page report.

2 Why Cubans Want to Leave

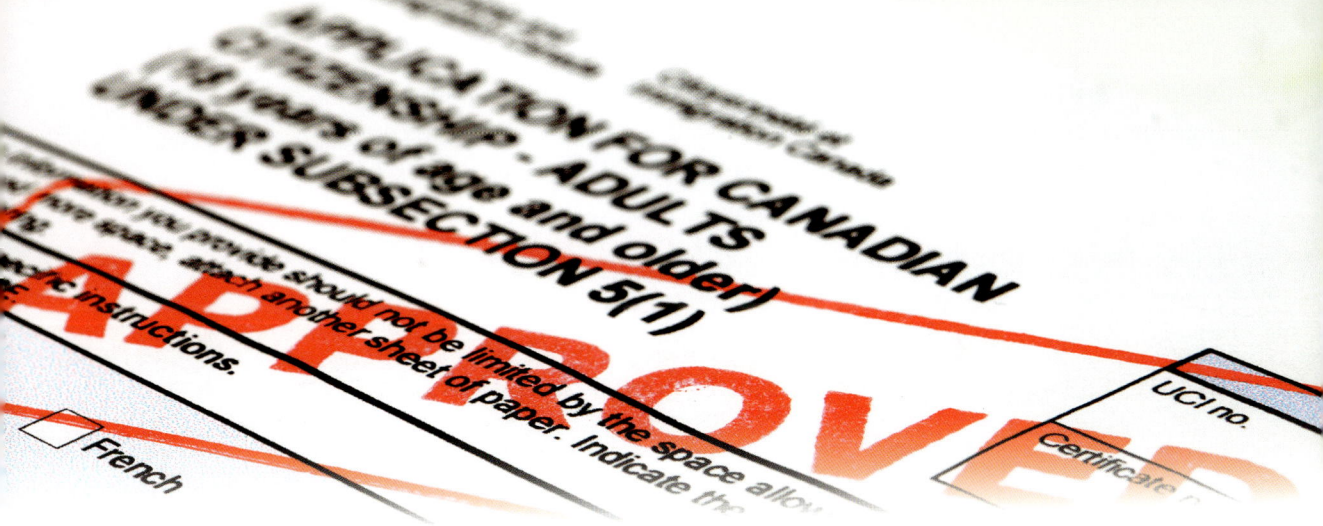

A dominant thread running through Cuban history is the continual search for freedom. For nearly two centuries, Cubans have come to North America to escape political instability and repressive governments in their homeland.

Yet nothing made more Cubans leave their country than Fidel Castro's ascension to power and the institution of his communist regime in 1959. More than one-tenth of the population has left since then, with most going to the United States. To understand what enabled Castro to take power, it is important to become familiar with Cuba's basic history.

The recorded history of Cuba began when Columbus landed on the eastern part of the island during his first voyage to the Americas in 1492. After Columbus' landing, the island became a colony of Spain. Spanish settlers founded the major cities, and their Cuban-born descendants populated the island over the next few centuries. When most of the original Amerindian population died from disease or from being overworked, the settlers brought slaves from Africa.

It was this mixture of African and Spanish influences that produced the Cuban people, but it took decades for a national identity to develop. From the 1500s until the early 1800s, most Cubans who were not enslaved thought of themselves as

◀ Cuban president Fidel Castro delivers a speech in Camagüey, Cuba, announcing victory in the communist revolution to oust dictator Fulgencio Batista, January 1959. More than one-tenth of the Cuban population has since escaped the repressive system to settle in another country.

Spaniards from Cuba. But the American Revolutionary War and the creation of an independent United States caused many Cubans to reflect on their own situation. Some began to see themselves as distinctly Cuban rather than as Spaniards living in Cuba. In addition, the American Revolution naturally raised the question of why Cubans, too, should not enjoy self-government. These feelings were intensified when Spanish colonial authorities forbade Cuban-born persons to hold high government office in their native land.

By the early 1800s many people living in Cuba were increasingly defining themselves as Cubans. They felt they were under the control of a foreign country, Spain, and that they had the right to freely govern themselves as a sovereign state. Eventually they decided that self-governance was worth fighting a war for.

The Fight for Independence

The 1850s saw the start of a struggle for freedom that, many Cubans say, has yet to be won. Spanish authorities put down several uprisings and conspiracies. Then in 1868 Cubans began the first of their wars of independence. The Ten Years' War, as it came to be called, ended in 1878 with the defeat of Cuban rebel forces—and tremendous devastation to the people and the econ-

Words to Understand in This Chapter

bodega—a grocery store that specializes in Hispanic foods.
communism—a political and economic system that advocates the elimination of private property, promotes the common ownership of goods, and typically insists that the Communist Party has sole authority to govern.
communist—a follower of communism; relating to or characteristic of communism.
dissidents—those who disagree with the established political system.
embargo—a government prohibition on trade with another country.
socialism—in communist theory, a stage of economic development that precedes full communism, during which society continues to include some inequality.

José Martí (1853–95), essayist and poet, was an illustrious leader in the Cuban fight for independence during the 1890s. He died fighting in the war against Spain, which began in 1895 and ended in 1898, just months after the United States entered the war on the side of Cuba.

omy. Nearly a quarter of a million people had been killed, and the large sugar estates on which the economy depended were in ruins.

When the war ended, Spain's government promised to permit more self-rule for Cubans, but it soon broke that promise. Cubans felt frustrated because their struggle for freedom had come to nothing. A new war broke out in 1895; it was largely inspired by the essayist and poet José Martí, a leading figure in Cuba's history.

Martí was killed in battle just weeks after the war began. Fighting dragged on for three years, and in 1898 the USS *Maine*, a battleship that had been sent to Cuba to protect American lives and property from the war's spreading violence, blew up in Havana harbor.

The United States blamed Spanish forces for the disaster and declared war on Spain. Cuban and American troops defeated the Spanish in a few months, ending four centuries of Spanish rule. The United States governed Cuba until May 20, 1902, when the Cuban flag was raised at Havana's ancient Morro Castle in a ceremony that signaled the birth of the independent Republic of Cuba. Many Cubans believed they had reached their goal of complete freedom, though they soon faced another letdown.

The Cuban Republic

Cuba was not yet completely independent because the U.S. government insisted that the Cuban constitution include the Platt Amendment, a clause that permitted Americans to intervene in the instance of a rebellion or revolution that the Cuban government could not control. Many Cubans resented the amendment, considering it an infringement of their sovereign rights.

The U.S. government intervened in Cuba several times—in 1906, 1912, and 1917—in response to the instability of the Cuban government and complaints of government corruption. However, Cuba showed promise in many ways: a middle class began to grow even in the midst of widespread unemployment. Also, Cuba had developed a free press, citizens were now free to speak out, and political parties competed for their vote. But the Cuban movement for democracy took a major blow in the early 1930s when Gerardo Machado, who had been elected president in 1924, refused to give up power and established a repressive dictatorship.

For the first time since the days of colonization, Cubans were imprisoned simply for disagreeing with the government, and political opponents were murdered by government thugs. Soon a new struggle for freedom began. After a general strike paralyzed the nation, Machado was overthrown in 1933. Fighting among political factions followed, until an army sergeant named Fulgencio Batista became de facto leader.

Batista made himself general and for the rest of the decade was the power behind puppet leaders. In 1934 the Platt Amendment, which had authorized the U.S. government to intervene in Cuban politics, was abolished (though the U.S. military did maintain control of a naval base at Guantánamo Bay, located on the island). The abolition of the amendment was very important to Cubans, because they could now say that they were no longer a quasi-colony subject to American political and military interference.

In 1940, under a new constitution, Batista ran for president and won. When his term ended four years later, he stepped down and made way for the elected democratic government of Ramón Grau San Martín, who was followed in 1948 by Carlos Prío Socarrás. Cubans believed that the freedom they had sought since colonial times had finally arrived.

Under Grau and Prío, the economy grew and democratic practices expanded. Cuba became one of Latin America's most economically advanced nations. But corrupt officials under both presidents stole millions of dollars that should have funded public services such as education and the road network. Using the need to end public corruption as an excuse to regain power, Batista ousted Prío in March 1952 in a *golpe de estado* (a coup, or sudden seizure of power) and made himself dictator.

Gerardo Machado (1871–1939) led Cuba in a time of government corruption and political chaos. During his dictatorship, which lasted from 1925 to 1933, Cubans began to migrate from the country to escape persecution as well as to search for better economic opportunities.

Many Cubans had been looking forward to the presidential election that year, with candidates promising to fight corruption, so they were angry to see their hopes of democracy dashed under Batista. In a democracy, citizens at least have the chance to elect new leaders, but Batista's new government permitted no elections or dissent. It censored newspapers and jailed political opponents. As under the Machado administration, government agents had a free hand to imprison or use direct force against those suspected of opposing Batista.

The Anti-Batista Resistance

A young lawyer named Fidel Castro was among those opposed

to Batista. In 1953 his forces assaulted a military barracks known as Moncada, in the eastern city of Santiago. The attack failed and Castro was imprisoned. But as part of a political amnesty that Batista granted political opponents two years later, Castro was released. He went to Mexico, where he organized another expedition against Batista.

In 1956 Castro and some 80 armed supporters landed on the eastern coast of Cuba. Batista's army hunted down most of the men, but a handful survived, including Castro, his brother Raúl, and Argentinean revolutionary Ernesto "Che" Guevara. The small group fled to the mountains of the Sierra Maestra to hide and regroup.

By this time, Batista had become so despised that a number of Cubans decided to help the tiny rebel army. Support grew in the Sierra Maestra as well as in the cities. Batista's own soldiers

Argentinean revolutionary Ernesto "Che" Guevara (right) fought alongside Fidel Castro (left) in the early stages of the Cuban Revolution. Following his six years of service in the Cuban government, Guevara led a guerrilla movement in Bolivia, where he was killed. Guevara became a mythic hero for Latin American communists.

were becoming demoralized, and a good number lost the desire to fight on the side of an unpopular dictator. Castro's men won several skirmishes over the next couple of years, putting Batista's army on the run. Finally, on New Year's Eve 1958, Batista gave up and fled the country. Castro and his army of revolutionaries entered Havana in triumph.

A week later, more than a million wildly cheering Cubans lined the streets to welcome the rebel army as it paraded through Havana. The vast majority of Cubans treated them like liberating heroes. They thought that, finally, after a century and a half of crushed dreams, Cuba was finally going to be free. They did not know that the new government would become a dictatorship that would impel a million Cubans to leave their homeland.

Cuba Under Castro

Ever since the days of fighting in the mountains against Batista's army, Fidel Castro had promised he would establish a stable democratic government free of corruption—a government that Cubans had always wanted but never had. Castro even traveled to Washington, D.C., in the spring of 1959 for a televised press conference to reassure his international audience of his democratic plan. "I know you are worried . . . first of all if we are communist," he stated in the address. "And of course . . . I have said very clearly that we are not communist." His words were a promise to many that the democratic, stable, and honest government that Cuba had needed for so long had finally arrived.

However, by the end of the year Castro had ousted most of the moderates from his government and replaced them with communists. In the following months, foreign as well as Cuban-owned businesses were expropriated, or taken by the government. Independent newspapers were shut down and replaced by government-owned newspapers that did not criticize Castro. People who protested were put in prison, and many were executed by firing squads.

In the aftermath of Castro's takeover, droves of Batista supporters fled to the United States. Most Cubans were glad Batista was gone. But as months passed and the Castro regime started to become more dictatorial, many well-to-do Cubans who had placed their hopes on the new government turned against it in disappointment and also fled north.

Cuba's world role was also changing. In May 1960, partly because of ideology and partly due to his resentment of the U.S. government, Castro established close relations with the communist Soviet Union, the United States' main adversary during the Cold War (a struggle for global influence that most historians date from 1947 to 1991). The Soviets began to sell arms to the Castro regime.

In January 1961, the United States severed diplomatic relations with Cuba. By that time, American plans to overthrow Castro were already under way. Over the years, the U.S. intelligence community would hatch numerous plots—including assassination attempts—to get rid of Castro. All, however, were unsuccessful.

Canada, however, maintained full diplomatic and trade relations with the Castro government. From the start of the Cuban Revolution, the successive administrations of the Canadian government took the stance that a policy of cooperation—as opposed to the American policy of confrontation—was best for the people of Cuba and Canada. Many Cuban exile groups were critical of that policy, arguing that Canada was obligated to speak out more against the regime's human rights violations.

From Dwight Eisenhower to George W. Bush, American presidents have consistently pursued policies designed to isolate Castro and Cuba. Finally, in 2014, President Barack Obama moved to start normalizing relations with Cuba.

Early attempts to remove Castro depended greatly on the efforts of Cuban exiles who were trained by the Central Intelligence Agency (CIA). On April 17, 1961, some 1,500 armed men of a Cuban-exile unit dubbed Brigade 2506 landed at the Bay of Pigs, in the Zapata Swamp of south-central Cuba. One of the Castro government's first responses was to immediately jail as many as 100,000 people suspected of giving support to Brigade 2506 in Havana and other cities. The government also mobilized the army to surround the invaders on a small beachhead. Although the exiles had already begun a bombing campaign with some successful results, President John F. Kennedy, under pressure from the international community, decided against ordering additional air strikes that might have broken Castro's encirclement. Brigade 2506 was defeated after three days of fighting.

For those who opposed Castro, the defeat at the Bay of Pigs was yet one more setback in Cuba's long struggle for freedom. Not long thereafter, Castro officially declared that his revolution

The Debate over Cuba

Cuban immigrants typically cite one of two main reasons for having left their country: political repression and economic hardship. The former motivated most of those who fled Cuba in the first quarter-century after Fidel Castro came to power. Since then, however, economics has been a larger factor in Cuban migration, experts say.

From the outset, the Castro government's human rights record was poor, according to Cuban refugee groups and independent organizations such as Amnesty International. The mistreatment of dissidents continued even after Fidel Castro stepped down and handed power to his younger brother, Raúl, in 2008. Nonetheless, the Cuban government has its defenders, both within and beyond the country's borders.

Castro supporters point out that after the revolution in 1959, the government set up free health care clinics, built new housing, and organized literacy campaigns to help more citizens read. In 2015, according to the United Nations Educational, Scientific and Cultural Organization (UNESCO), Cuba boasted the highest literacy rate among all Latin American countries--and one of the highest rates in the entire world. Its child mortality rate, according to World Health Organization data, is lower than that of the United States.

The counterargument critics make is that Cuba had already been among the region's most advanced countries *before* Castro's takeover. By the 1940s and 1950s, Cuba ranked among the top three or four countries in Latin America in terms of literacy rate, infant mortality rate, and ownership of cars, telephones, and television sets. Critics also call attention to countries such as Costa Rica and Uruguay, small nations that remained among the most advanced in Latin America without eliminating political freedoms as Cuba did.

Cuban militiamen and members of the Revolutionary Army celebrate their victory over the Cuban exiles. The Bay of Pigs Invasion in April 1961 ended in failure and was a major setback in the long campaign to end Castro's regime.

was communist, and that he himself was, in his words, "a Marxist-Leninist until the day I die." The United States responded to Castro's declaration and his general policies by imposing a trade embargo.

What many Cubans feared most had come true. Oppression was now practiced more in the open than ever. Political prisoners filled Cuba's jails, but they were not the only ones vulnerable to persecution. Simply not showing enthusiastic support for the government often meant the loss of a job or harassment by government-sponsored mobs. By 1962, nearly 200,000 Cubans had escaped the dictatorship, most of them resettling in the United States.

The steady flow of migration was cut off, however, by the Cuban Missile Crisis of October 1962. That month U.S. satellite photos showed that the Soviet Union was building nuclear missile sites in Cuba. President Kennedy demanded the sites be dismantled immediately and ordered a naval blockade of the island. For the next two weeks, the world found itself on the brink of nuclear war.

But the Soviets backed down. They dismantled the bases in exchange for American concessions, including a promise by the United States that it would not allow any more exile invasions of Cuba. In addition, direct flights between Cuba and the United States were brought to a halt, making it much more difficult for Castro's opponents to leave. It was not until 1965 that flights resumed. By then, Castro had secured a strong hold over the Cuban people. He organized Committees for the Defense of the Revolution in neighborhoods to spy on and harass those frustrated with the regime. Citizens were also required to "volunteer" on farms; those who did not show up to work were at risk of not having any employment.

A Communist Cuba

With the communization of Cuba, everyone worked for the government; even small retail shops—the pharmacy down the street, the corner bodega—had been taken over by the regime in what was called the "Great Revolutionary Offensive." Only the government was permitted to own businesses. As the years went on, the regime maintained its restrictions and continued to send dissidents to jail, where conditions were terrible. The most famous political prisoners, called the *plantados* (roughly meaning "the ones who stood their ground"), lived for years in tiny cells, wearing nothing but their underwear and surviving on meager rations of rotten meat and spoiled beans.

The Cuban government's influence grew beyond the island during the 1960s. The Castro government sent advisers to instruct communist guerrillas fighting in several Latin American countries. None of these revolutionary groups was able to take power except in Nicaragua, where a group known as the Sandinistas ousted the dictator Anastasio Somoza and set up a socialist state modeled on Castro's Cuba. For most of the 1980s, the Sandinistas were Cuba's principal ally in Latin America.

Cuban foreign influence extended beyond the Americas, though. In the 1970s and 1980s, Castro sent troops overseas to fight alongside pro-communist rebels in Angola, Ethiopia, and other parts of Africa. He also sent military advisers to support the government in Nicaragua when a group of U.S.–backed anti-Sandinista guerrillas known as the contras rose in arms.

Despite Cuba's growing international influence, however, economic troubles plagued the country. There were food shortages, which the government attributed to the U.S. embargo, but which Castro's critics blamed on the regime's mismanagement of agriculture and manufacturing. Whatever the case, nearly all consumer items—from clothing to soap to basic food staples—were rationed. Every Cuban family was issued a ration book that severely limited how much it could buy each month. As of 2016, this rationing system remained in operation.

The Refugee Crises

In April 1980, in response to an incident involving asylum seekers at the Peruvian embassy in Havana, the Castro regime abruptly lifted restrictions on leaving the country. Over the next few months, more than 125,000 people left the island in boats and headed to Florida in what became known as the Mariel boatlift.

In the wake of the Mariel exodus, organizations such as Americas Watch, Amnesty International, and the United Nations Human Rights Commission began to issue reports documenting the poor human rights conditions in Cuba. Their findings were a blow to the international prestige of Castro's regime.

Cuba's standing got worse in the late 1980s and early 1990s with the collapse of communism in Eastern Europe and the breakup of the Soviet Union. Soviet subsidies to Cuba were dramatically reduced and ultimately discontinued entirely. This put the Cuban economy in even deeper trouble. The situation encouraged more Cubans, including the young generation who only knew life under Castro, to leave. In 1994 tens of thousands left Cuba in homemade rafts—an exodus that came to be known as the "rafter" crisis.

Because this major exodus was proof of the people's discontent, the Cuban government felt pressured to relax some of its stringent economic rules. It encouraged tourism from Western nations, legalized the use of U.S. currency (previously, Cubans were prosecuted for having American money), and permitted the operation of a number of privately owned businesses, most of which were tourist-related. But Cubans were angered that they were not permitted to enter the finest restaurants, resorts, and stores, which were reserved for foreigners who did not need rationing cards. And though the government's regulation of the economy was less rigid during this time, there was no move toward reforming Cuba's politically oppressive laws. New legislation passed in the early 1990s established even tougher penalties for criticizing the regime.

The next major crisis occurred in 1996 when Cuban air force jets shot down two civilian planes flown by members of Brothers to the Rescue, a Miami-based exile group that flew over the Florida Straits looking for lost rafters. In response to the attacks, the U.S. government passed legislation that tightened the embargo and ensured that it would remain in place for some time.

The Question of Dissent

Also adding to the dissatisfaction of Cuban dissenters—and to their desire to leave—was the government's decision to ignore the advice of Pope John Paul II, which he offered during his January 1998 visit to Cuba. The first pope to visit Cuba called for "the world to open up to Cuba, and for Cuba to open up to the world." Despite the protests of international leaders and activist organizations, dissidents who called for peaceful change in Cuba continued to be harassed, jailed, and fired from their jobs.

The persistence and seriousness of Castro's repressive measures convinced Canada to reconsider its foreign policy with Cuba. Beginning in the late 1990s, the Canadian government acknowledged that its policy of engagement with Castro had not improved

Some of the more than 125,000 refugees who participated in the Mariel boatlift of 1980 celebrate their safe arrival at Eglin Airforce Base, Florida. The refugees arrived over the course of six months, following Castro's sudden decision to lift restrictions on emigration.

Cuba's human rights record after four decades, and Canada issued more criticisms of the Cuban government, in bilateral talks as well as in international forums. In addition, Canada began voting to censure Cuba at the annual UN Human Rights Commission meetings in Geneva. Nonetheless, Canada never broke trade or diplomatic relations with Cuba, and it continued to speak out against the U.S. trade embargo.

In 2002 an initiative called the Varela Project sought to pressure the Cuban government to make democratic reforms. It was the brainchild of Oswaldo Payá Sardiñas, an engineer-turned-activist who in 1988 had cofounded the Movimiento Cristiano Liberación (Christian Liberation Movement), or MCL. MCL advocated peaceful change "by the Cuban people and for the Cuban people" that would lead to a more open, socially just, and democratic Cuba. With the Varela Project, Payá hoped to take advantage of a provision in the Cuban constitution that empowered citizens to propose laws. The provision required the signatures of at least 10,000 eligible voters. By mid-2002, having exceeded that threshold, the Varela Project petitioned the government to hold a referendum on laws that would guarantee freedom of speech, freedom of assembly, and freedom of the press; mandate the release of political prisoners; allow candidates from parties other than the Communist Party of Cuba to run for political office; and permit the establishment of privately owned businesses.

In response to the Varela Project's petition, the regime mobilized government-affiliated groups to mount a rival petition drive. The government claimed that more than 99 percent of Cuba's eligible voters signed a petition reaffirming the country's commitment to socialism. Then, in late June 2002, Cuba's legislature—the National Assembly of People's Power—took up the question. After several days of speeches denouncing opponents of the government and extolling the virtues of Cuba's system, the National Assembly voted unanimously to pass a constitutional amendment making socialism "irrevocable." The Varela Project's petition for a referendum was rejected.

But the effort had attracted international attention. Oswaldo Payá was awarded the European Parliament's Sakharov Prize for Freedom of Thought. In a move that surprised many observers, the Cuban government permitted Payá to travel to Europe in December 2002 to accept the award.

"Many people have linked this prize to the Varela Project, and rightly so, since the thousands of Cubans who, in the midst of repression, have signed the petition calling for a referendum are making a decisive contribution to bringing about the changes which Cuba needs," Payá declared in accepting the Sakharov Prize on behalf of all Cubans.

> Those changes would mean involvement in cultural and economic life, civil and political rights, and national reconciliation. That would constitute a genuine exercise in self-determination by our people. We must reject the myth that we Cubans have to live without rights in order to support our country's independence and sovereignty.... [I]ndependence and national sovereignty are inseparable from the exercise of basic rights. We Cubans—whether we live in Cuba or in the diaspora—are a single people and we have both the determination and the ability to build a just, free and democratic society, without hatred and without the desire for

revenge. In the words of José Marti, "With everyone and for everyone's benefit."

Crackdown and Backlash

The Cuban government soon moved to clamp down on pro-democracy activists. In March 2003 it arrested more than 75 dissidents, including Varela Project organizers, independent journalists, and Cubans who ran home libraries containing books the government claimed were subversive. Payá—probably because of his international stature—wasn't among those arrested. In early April the arrested dissidents were summarily tried and convicted. Most received long prison sentences.

On the eve of the trials, a Cuban airliner was hijacked and forced to land in Florida by a Cuban seeking asylum in the United States for himself and his wife and child. That same day, three Cubans commandeered a ferry in Havana Bay and attempted to sail it to Florida. The ship ran out of fuel in international waters and was ultimately returned to Cuba, where the hijackers were executed.

Cuba's foreign minister, Felipe Pérez Roque, attempted to blame the United States for the hijackings and for the recent calls for change in Cuba. The Varela Project organizers and other human-rights activists who'd been convicted were "mercenaries at the service of the [American] empire," according to Pérez.

> After more than 40 years of an ironclad economic, financial and commercial blockade, of aggressions, terrorist acts, more than 600 assassination attempts on the life of the Cuban President; after decades of incitement to subversion, illegal emigration, sabotage, activities by armed groups whose acts of terrorism against our country have been tolerated in the country where they originate; after all that history, which our people know only too well having suffered the loss of many lives and considerable material losses—the blockade alone has cost Cuba more than $70 billion USD—on top of all that, our people have had to contend with the obsession of U.S. governments to fabricate an opposition in Cuba, to fabricate an organized dissidence in Cuba, to foment in Cuba the emergence or strengthening of groups responding to their interests, with an evidently annexationist vision, those who would be responsible some day for propitiating Cuba's annexation to the United States, in the supposed scenario of the defeat of the Cuban Revolution. That has been its obsession and the purpose of the laws, the funding, the incitement and the role of the special services.
>
> One plan after another has foundered against the unity of our people, against the moral authority of the Cuban Revolution, against the unquestionable

> fact that the overwhelming majority of the Cuban people support and defend the Revolution, against the unquestionable historical moral leadership of the Cuban Revolution. They have come up against all of that, but they have not overcome that resistance, which has elicited international admiration.

The Cuban government's crackdown on dissenters certainly didn't elicit "international admiration." Rather, it produced significant blowback from the international community. In June 2003 the European Union imposed diplomatic sanctions on Cuba. The following year, the UN Human Rights Commission passed a resolution condemning the Castro regime's violations of its citizens' basic rights.

For its part, the United States in 2004 increased restrictions on Cuban Americans wishing to visit family members on the island. More significantly, U.S. rules regarding remittances (money sent from abroad) to Cuba were tightened. Previously, Cuban Americans were allowed to send cash to any household in Cuba—provided the household didn't include a high-level government official or a high-level member of the Communist Party—and authorized travelers to Cuba were permitted to distribute up to $3,000 in remittances. Under the new regulations, Cuban Americans were limited to $300 in remittances per quarter, and only immediate family members could receive the money; authorized travelers could carry just $300 in remittance money.

Cuba's economy, already foundering from a downturn in tourism, was hit hard by the new U.S. restrictions. Castro compounded the problems by prohibiting Cubans from using American currency (many Cubans had come to rely on the U.S. dollar for ordinary transactions) and by imposing a 10 percent tax on dollars converted to Cuban pesos. The result was additional economic hardship for Cuba's people. The hardship only increased after July 2005, when a powerful hurricane devastated the island.

Change in Leadership

In July 2006 Fidel Castro underwent surgery for what the Cuban government described as gastrointestinal bleeding. In the months

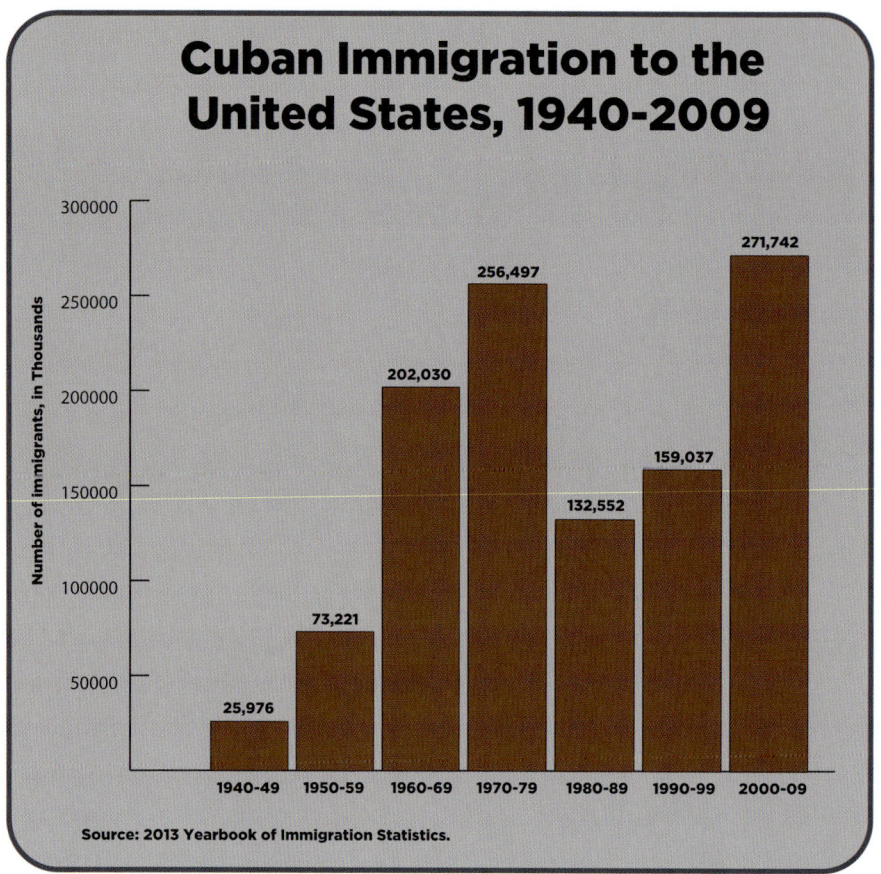

that followed, he was noticeably absent from public events. Eventually Castro admitted, in a letter read on Cuban state TV in December 2007, that he didn't plan to remain in power indefinitely. The following February he resigned. The 81-year-old Castro had been Cuba's president for 49 years.

Fidel Castro's 76-year-old brother, Raúl, was elevated to the presidency. He'd been Cuba's acting leader since Fidel Castro first fell ill. During that time, Raúl Castro had broached the possibility of "structural and conceptual reforms" in Cuba, as well as better relations with the United States. However, his brother had quickly put a damper on such ideas, announcing that the circumstances weren't right for major policy shifts. Now, with Raúl Castro's authority solidified, some international observers anticipated significant changes in Cuba.

President George W. Bush believed the United States and the

international community could play a useful role in encouraging a transition to democracy in Cuba. "The international community should work with the Cuban people to begin to build institutions that are necessary for democracy," Bush declared. "And eventually, this transition ought to lead to free and fair elections—and I mean free and I mean fair, not these kind of staged elections that the Castro brothers try to foist off as being true democracy. And we're going to help—the United States will help the people of Cuba realize the blessings of liberty."

Raúl Castro proved to be in no hurry to usher in democratic political reforms. But the new Cuban leader moved quickly to implement economic reforms. By the summer of 2008—just half a year since assuming the presidency—Castro had announced that farmers would be able to cultivate more land privately. He'd also decided to end the policy of paying everyone the same salary. Now, workers and managers who met production goals would be eligible for bonuses. These reforms were clearly designed to bolster Cuba's flagging economy by giving individuals an incentive for greater productivity. According to many analysts, the moves demonstrated that Raúl Castro was more pragmatic than his older brother. He was willing to jettison the strict communist principles that had guided Cuban economic policy since the triumph of the revolution in 1959.

But, given the depth of Cuba's economic problems, the reforms proved no panacea. In fact, according to the Cuban government, 2008 was the worst year for the nation's economy since 1991, when the collapse of the Soviet Union ended that country's generous subsidies to its communist ally. Cuba's problems were made worse by two hurricanes, Gustav and Ike, which hit the island in rapid succession in August and September 2008. The storms devastated crops and left about 200,000 Cubans homeless.

Economic Reforms and Political Repression

In April 2009 the new U.S. president, Barack Obama, announced several policy changes regarding Cuba. He removed the restrictions imposed by his predecessor on Cuban Americans' visits to family members on the island, and on their remittances to family members. Obama said this would "help bridge the gap among divided Cuban families and promote the freer flow of information and humanitarian items to the Cuban people," which he believed would ultimately begin to "foster the beginnings of grassroots democracy on the island."

The president further relaxed travel restrictions to Cuba in 2011. The new rules allowed American students, members of church groups, and people traveling with cultural organizations to visit Cuba legally. Ordinary American tourists, however, were still prohibited from traveling to the island.

Meanwhile, Raúl Castro's economic reforms continued. In 2010 Castro announced plans to dramatically scale back government jobs in favor of private-sector employment. The following year, a new law was passed allowing Cubans to buy and sell private property for the first time in half a century.

But the Castro regime continued to suppress dissent, according to rights-monitoring groups in Cuba and international organizations such as Human Rights Watch. The regime did release many political prisoners—for example, all of those sentenced in 2003 in conjunction with the crackdown on Project Varela had been freed by 2011. In addition, long prison sentences were handed down less frequently to critics of the government. However, those developments appeared to reflect a shift in the regime's tactics rather than a genuine commitment to increasing political freedoms. "The government," noted a Human Rights Watch report, "increasingly relied on arbitrary arrests and short-term detentions to restrict the basic rights of its critics, including the right to assemble and move about freely. Cuba's government also pressured dissidents to choose between exile and continued repression or even imprisonment, leading scores to leave the country with their families during 2011."

The Castro regime's most famous critic, Oswaldo Payá, was offered the chance to go into exile, but he refused. That refusal would cost the MCL and Varela Project leader his life. In July

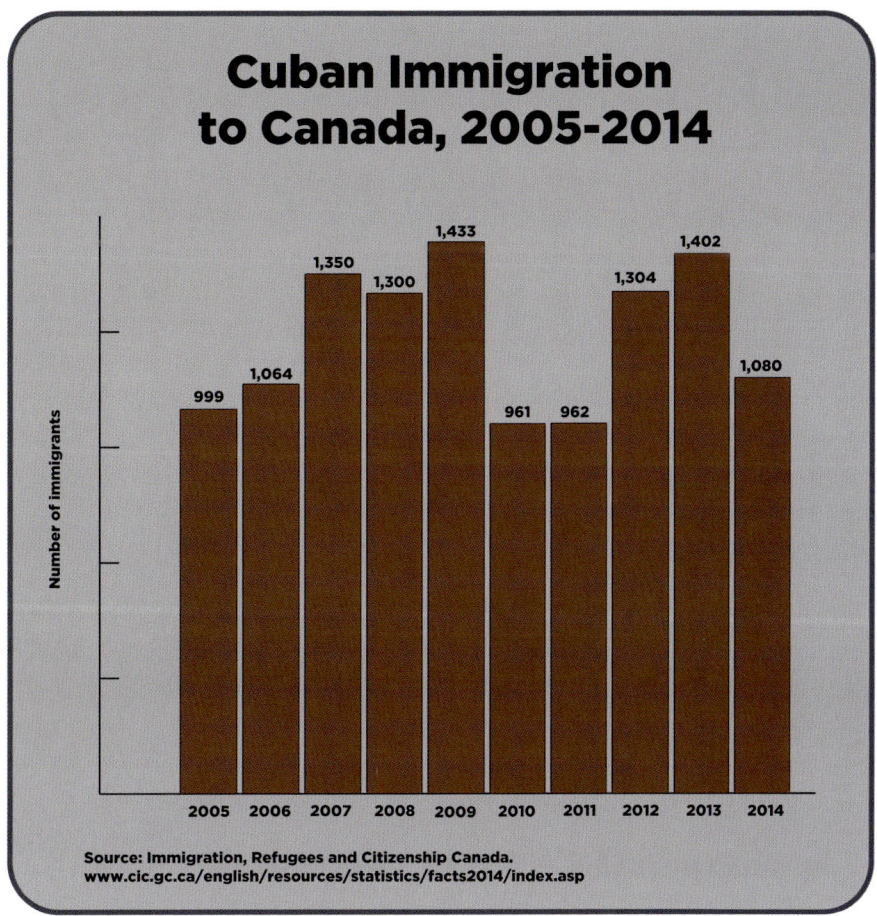

2012 Payá and another Cuban dissident, Harold Cepero, were killed after a car in which they were passengers crashed in the eastern province of Granma. The Cuban government claimed the crash was an accident caused by the recklessness of the car's driver, Spanish lawyer and activist Ángel Carromero. But Carromero, who survived the wreck, said that the car had been rammed and run off the road by a vehicle driven by Cuban security officers. He believed Payá and Cepero had been alive when they were taken from the wreck and had been murdered while in official custody.

The United States joined other countries, as well as the Payá family, in calling for an independent investigation into the circumstances surrounding the dissidents' deaths. However, the Castro regime didn't permit such an inquiry to take place.

Why Cubans Want to Leave

President Barack Obama shakes hands with President Raúl Castro of Cuba during the Summit of the Americas at the Atlapa Convention Center in Panama City, Panama, April 11, 2015.

A New Era in U.S.-Cuban Relations?

In late 2012 the Castro regime ended a policy it had long used to stop Cuban citizens from leaving the island: the requirement that an exit permit be purchased by anyone wishing to travel abroad. Costing the equivalent of more than a year's salary for the average state worker, the permits were far too expensive for most people to afford. Even without exit permits, overseas travel remained beyond the financial means of many Cubans (and highly trained professionals such as doctors and engineers needed the government's permission to leave the island). Nonetheless, the new rules gave more Cubans the opportunity to go abroad. Of course, prospective travelers would be subject to any requirements or restrictions set by the destination country.

In December 2014—after a year and a half of secret negotiations brokered by Pope Francis—Barack Obama and Raúl Castro announced an agreement to begin normalizing relations between their respective countries. The deal eased U.S. restrictions on commerce with Cuba. However, it didn't formally end the trade embargo. Only Congress could authorize that step—and Congress showed little inclination to do so.

During the summer of 2015, Cuba and the United States reopened embassies that had been shuttered since 1961. The Cuban embassy in Washington, D.C., opened its doors on July 20; less than a month later, on August 14, the American flag was raised over the U.S. embassy in Havana for the first time in more than 54 years.

In spite of the substantial easing of U.S.-Cuba tensions, most observers predicted that the relationship between the two countries would continue to be marked by difficulties and disagreements. "This milestone does not signify an end to the many differences that still separate our governments," John Kerry, the U.S. secretary of state, said after Cuba opened its embassy in Washington, D.C. "But it does reflect the reality that the cold war ended long ago and that the interests of both countries are better served by engagement than by estrangement."

 ## Text-Dependent Questions

1. Which European country ruled Cuba from the 16th century to the end of the 19th century?
2. Name the dictator who seized power in Cuba in 1952 and who was overthrown seven years later.
3. Who was Oswaldo Payá?

 ## Research Project

Use a library or the Internet to find out Cuba's five largest cities and their respective populations. List them in a table, from largest to smallest. Locate the cities on a map of Cuba.

3 A History of Cuban Migration

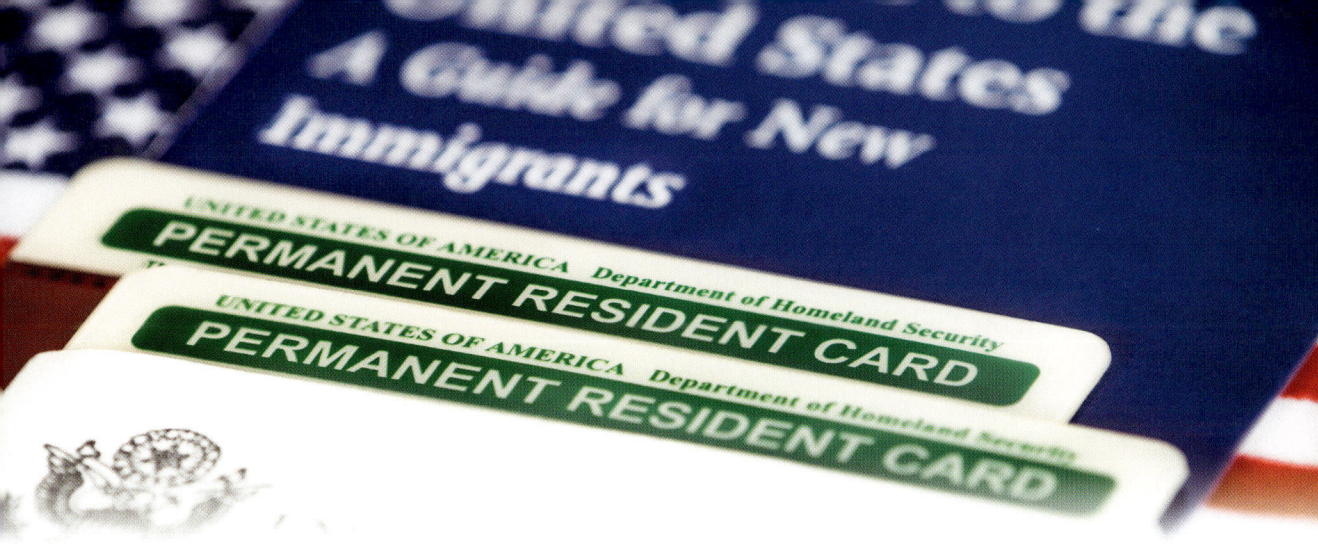

In 2012, according to the Pew Research Center, Cubans constituted the third-largest Hispanic group in the United States, numbering approximately 2 million. That figure included exiles, their American-born descendants, as well as Cuban Americans whose families had settled in the United States before Castro took power. The Cuban presence in continental North America actually predates the founding of the United States by more than two centuries.

Cubans in North America

Cubans lived in Florida when it was a colony of Spain, from the 1500s to 1821. In that year, the territory of Florida was sold to the United States, then still a young nation. Many Cubans made their home in St. Augustine, the oldest European settlement in what is now the United States. The settlement's imposing fortress, Castillo San Marcos, was designed by a Cuban engineer named Ignacio Daza and constructed under the direction of Laureano de Torres y Ayala, one of the three Cuban-born governors in Spanish Florida's history. A garrison of troops defended its 12-foot walls, and with the help of an armada that sailed from Havana under the Cuban-born general Esteban Berroa, it

◀ For decades Cubans have attempted the often dangerous journey to Florida in all kinds of vessels—in this case, a 1951 Chevrolet truck. The makeshift boat was apprehended by the U.S. Coast Guard, and all 12 passengers were repatriated to Cuba.

turned back a British attempt to conquer St. Augustine in 1702. A second attack in 1740 also failed.

Cubans were active during the American Revolutionary War as well. In 1779 Cuban troops under Spanish field marshal Bernardo de Gálvez forced the British out of a line of forts that stretched along the Gulf of Mexico. Two years later, Gálvez and his troops reconquered Pensacola, Florida, with the help of yet another armada from Havana led by the Cuban Juan Manuel de Cagigal. The victory meant redcoats were pinned down who would have otherwise been mobilized against the Continental army in Virginia at the Battle of Yorktown. These soldiers' absence made even more certain the British defeat in the war's final battle.

Cubans played a key role in that decisive battle as well. With the Continental army running out of money and on the verge of mutiny, George Washington asked a French admiral, the comte de Grasse, for help. De Grasse sailed to Havana and with the help of Cagigal—the new governor of Cuba—convinced residents of Havana to donate an estimated 1.2 million French livres to Washington's army. It was enough to supply troops with the weapons, munitions, and uniforms they needed to defeat the British.

The 19th century brought a change in Cuba's self-image as well as in its attitude toward the United States. In the preceding century, Cubans had helped the United States gain independence from Great Britain; now, inspired by the American Revolution,

Words to Understand in This Chapter

armada—a fleet of warships.
indoctrinate—to teach a person or group to accept a set of ideas uncritically, with the goal of discouraging independent thought.
Marielito—a Cuban who immigrated to the United States during the 1980 Mariel boatlift.
nationalize—to transfer a privately run business or industry to state control.

An 18th-century engraving of St. Augustine, Florida, the oldest European settlement in America. Many Cubans had lived in the colony of Florida before the Spanish sold it to the United States in 1821.

Cubans sought help from the United States to gain their own independence from Spain. In the first decades of the 19th century, there were armed uprisings as well as peaceful attempts at political reform, but all of them failed, as Spanish authorities cracked down on dissenters. Beginning in the 1820s, Cubans fleeing this political repression started to arrive in America.

Some exiles went to Key West, Florida, where by 1831 there was a Cuban-owned cigar factory in operation. New Orleans, too, had a small Cuban community. But most Cubans of the period settled in New York City, where for several decades they organized to fight for Cuban independence. The best-known leader of the period was Narciso López. In 1848 he established contacts with pro-slavery American Southerners who hoped to take Cuba from Spain and annex it as a slave state. They helped finance an expedition led by López in 1850. The expedition went from Florida to Cuba with 600 armed Cuban exiles and American soldiers. López and his men took the town of Cárdenas and held it for one day, until Spanish troops counter-

The flag of Cuba was created by independence leader Narcisco López in 1849. Its horizontal stripes and color pattern was inspired by the design of the U.S. flag.

attacked and forced them to sail back to Florida. He led a second expedition the following year, but was captured and executed by Spanish authorities.

Exiles continued to orchestrate an independence movement in the United States well into the 1870s, as the Ten Years' War raged in Cuba. The rebels even had representatives ask the administration of President Ulysses S. Grant for help in the war against Spain. The representatives were turned down, but nevertheless, Cubans kept coming to America.

Gradually, the Cuban community in New York grew large enough to form small but well-established neighborhoods in the Lower East Side. There were Cuban restaurants, newspapers, bodegas, and at least one Cuban-owned Spanish-language bookstore. Around the same period, the small community in Key West grew as large as the one in New York. In 1875, the city even elected a Cuban American mayor, and in the 1880s, it sent two representatives to Florida's state legislature. A decade later Cuban cigar manufacturers founded Ybor City, the oldest neighborhood in what is now Tampa.

Cubans living in America had a pivotal role in waging the

1895 War of Independence. The revolution was led by José Martí, a poet and a national hero. Martí arrived in New York City in 1880 after being deported from Cuba for his pro-independence activities. While living in New York, he wrote some of his most famous poems and also worked as an art critic for the *New York Sun*.

But the struggle for an independent Cuba was Martí's principal motivation. When he first got to New York he found a Cuban community still demoralized from defeat in the Ten Years' War, which had ended two years earlier. He organized rallies throughout Manhattan, renewing the call for independence and urging fellow exiles to unite. The speeches he delivered have become famous in Cuban history.

Martí's pro-independence activities continued for a decade. In 1891 he first visited the booming communities of Key West and Tampa, home to perhaps 10,000 Cubans. The locals welcomed him as a hero, as the great hope for a free Cuba. His next years were spent traveling between New York and Florida to raise funds, buy arms, recruit troops, and organize the leadership

Father Varela and the Early Cuban Americans

One of the most famous of the early Cubans in America was Félix Varela, a philosopher and Catholic priest who founded *El Habanero*, a pro-independence, anti-slavery newspaper. It was the first regularly issued Spanish-language publication in the United States.

The Cuban independence movement in America struggled to find a single cause that everyone could support. Some exiles sought outright independence for Cuba, others preferred to remain a part of the Spanish empire but with more self-rule, and a third group wanted Cuba to become a U.S. state. Father Varela grew frustrated with the bickering of various factions and with Spain's unwillingness to accept reform of any kind, and so he decided to shift his attention toward his priestly duties.

Varela founded a school for children of the poverty-stricken Irish immigrants who lived in Manhattan's most infamous 19th-century slum, the Five Corners. During the cholera epidemic of 1832, he set up a medical center for victims hospitals refused to treat. His dedication to the immigrants earned him the title "the Vicar of the Irish." Varela died in 1848. A U.S. postage stamp in his honor was issued in 1997.

for a new rebellion. When everything was ready, he gave the order and Cuba's War of Independence began on February 24, 1895. Martí landed in Cuba that April, but was killed in battle five weeks later.

Republican Years

Cuba won independence from Spain in 1898 and was granted sovereignty from the U.S. administration in 1902. In its formative period as a republic, Cuba suffered through corrupt governments that were hard-pressed to revitalize a country beset by years of warfare. Cubans continued to immigrate to the United States. Until Gerardo Machado became dictator in 1925, most were primarily seeking economic opportunities. During the Machado dictatorship, however, the motivation for leaving Cuba tended to be more political—civilians were fleeing persecution and opposition leaders were seeking a safe place where they could plan their next move. Former president Mario García Menocal and future president Carlos Mendieta were among those who lived temporarily in the United States while plotting the overthrow of Machado, which took place in 1933.

In the two decades that followed, stability returned to Cuba, and Cubans who migrated to the United States were motivated mainly by economic considerations. But political repression began to once again drive Cubans out with the reemergence of Fulgencio Batista in 1952. This former army sergeant had been the country's behind-the-scenes ruler during the 1930s. When he overthrew elected Carlos Prío, the elected president, in 1952, Batista initiated another period of corruption and misrule.

Throughout the rest of the 1950s, Cuban leaders in the United States resumed the tradition of plotting to overthrow tyranny in their homeland. Prío was arrested by federal authorities on charges of conspiracy to smuggle arms, and a young man named Fidel Castro traveled to Cuban communities along the East Coast, raising funds to arm his own anti-Batista group. In 1956 Prío met Castro secretly in Texas, and he pledged to provide enough funds for an armed landing.

It was with that landing, which took place in December 1956, that Castro and his group began the fight that ended with Batista's fall on January 1, 1959. The government Castro established soon became dictatorial too, which brought about the first mass Cuban exodus to the United States.

The Castro Years and the Golden Exiles

The exiles of the Castro era would come in four different waves, each with distinct demographic characteristics. Cubans in the first wave would be dubbed the "Golden Exiles." They were mostly members of Cuba's pre-Castro elite and its educated middle class, and they arrived between the beginning of the revolution and the mid-1960s.

The next wave included passengers of what were known as

The dictatorship of Fulgencia Batista during the 1950s marked a difficult period of government corruption and misrule for Cuba, and initiated another wave of Cuban exiles looking to escape political repression.

A History of Cuban Migration 51

the Freedom Flights, which ran between 1965 and 1973. Many individuals of this wave were small-business owners, factory workers, or farmers. The next major group arrived in a period of just five months in 1980, during the Mariel boatlift. They were largely working-class people, but some of the exiles were the first professionals educated under the Castro regime to migrate. There were more non-white Cubans among the Marielitos than in previous waves. The fourth wave began in 1994 with the "rafter" crisis, and was largely made up of young men and women who were born after 1959 and lived their entire lives under Castro's rule.

People with ties to the Batista regime were the first to leave after the triumph of Castro's rebel army. Some 3,000 government officials, soldiers, policemen, and business people with links to the old dictatorship fled the island during the first few weeks of 1959. The regime they served was so unpopular that the vast majority of Cubans were happy to see them leave.

But it did not take long for a group of Cubans who had supported Castro in the revolution to become disenchanted with the system he was working to establish. After the revolutionary government began to curb freedoms and nationalize businesses, the educated elite decided conditions were so intolerable they had to leave.

Nearly 260,000 of the Golden Exiles left between 1959 and 1962. An overwhelming number of these immigrants were Cuba's leading men and women in the professional and business sectors. A study undertaken in 1963 by Stanford University found that 7.8 percent of the Golden Exiles had been lawyers, while the most recent census prior to the study, taken in 1953, reported that lawyers comprised only 0.5 percent of Cuba's population. Another 34 percent of the group were classed as "professional or managerial," compared to 9 percent of Cuba's population. And more than a third had a high school or college degree, compared to 4 percent of all Cubans.

The education and high income of these Cuban newcomers made them different from many immigrants who had come to the United States in decades past. In the 19th century, the majority of those who left Poland, Italy, Ireland, Germany, and other countries were driven by economic motives, hoping that in the United States they could find work opportunities that were difficult to find back home. Cubans, on the other hand, left their country primarily for political reasons. They preferred to be thought of as "exiles" or "refugees" and not "immigrants" because the former terms conveyed that they had indeed fled political repression. Nestor Carbonell, an exile of this wave who later became an executive at Pepsi-Cola, wrote of the Golden Exiles: "We did not come as immigrants pulled by the American economic dream, but as refugees pushed by the Cuban political nightmare."

What motivated many exiles during these early years was not the traditional immigrant desire to rebuild lives in a new country, but a zeal to overthrow the dictatorship that ruled their beloved homeland. And because they believed ousting Castro would take a short time, they expected they would live in America only temporarily and would return to Cuba after Castro's removal. Consequently, in the beginning they paid less attention to rebuilding shattered careers or reestablishing lost businesses than to fighting the regime in Havana. Soon many anti-Castro groups—some of whom were rivals—sprang up.

Among the Golden Exiles was a military group that with U.S. assistance launched the failed Bay of Pigs invasion. It was by far the largest and best-known anti-Castro operation.

Throughout late 1961 and into 1962, exile groups conducted hit-and-run guerrilla operations against military targets in Cuba. The agenda of the Golden Exiles was disrupted in 1962 with the Cuban Missile Crisis in October. The United States discovered that the Soviet Union was installing nuclear missiles in Cuba. President Kennedy demanded their removal, and the Soviets eventually backed down, avoiding a possible nuclear war.

But the end of the crisis brought repercussions for the Cuban exiles. An agreement between the U.S. and Soviet governments stated that no more exile raids on Cuba would be launched from American soil. It also stated that all direct scheduled flights between Cuba and the United States would end. From that point on, any Cuban who wanted to leave would have to first ask permission to go to a third country—most often, Spain or Mexico—and from there apply for a visa to enter the United States.

This dramatically slowed the flow of Cubans to America. Only about 15,000 arrived in 1963, and the same number arrived in 1964, compared to the more than 75,000 who arrived in the first nine months of 1962, before the October missile crisis. Many Cubans who could not get permission from the government to leave decided to escape illegally, crossing the dangerous Florida Straits in boats or rafts made of inner tubes. Tens of thousands more would do the same in the coming years.

Soon enough discontent built up in Cuba, and Castro decided to finally give potential defectors the opportunity to leave voluntarily. In late September 1965, he declared that the northern port of Camarioca would be open to anyone who wanted to make the crossing to the United States.

Freedom Flights

In the weeks following Castro's decision to open Camarioca, Cubans in Miami rented just about anything that could float and headed to the port to bring waiting relatives to the United States. Nearly 5,000 arrived in all manner of seacraft—leaky sailboats, trawlers, tugboats. The exodus became so chaotic that the Cuban and American governments negotiated for the resumption of flights to the United States. The decision marked the beginning of the Vuelos de la Libertad (Freedom Flights).

Although the Castro government allowed the flights, it also placed restrictions on who was permitted to leave. Several categories of skilled workers and professionals deemed essential to Cuba had to remain in the country. Those who applied to leave had their property confiscated and were forced to spend months working on farms while waiting their turn to fly out of the country.

The Freedom Flights began in December 1965 and ended in April 1973. Approximately 250,000 Cubans flew to America during those years, and by the end of the period, the Cuban-born population of the United States had grown to more than half a million.

Because of the occupation-based restrictions Castro put in place for this second wave of exiles, the group was in many ways different from the Golden Exiles. A large segment consisted of small-business owners, factory workers, and farmers. Only 12 percent had jobs described as "professional or managerial," compared to 34 percent among Golden Exiles. In a 1980 study, 57 percent of Freedom Flights arrivals were said to be "blue collar, service or agricultural workers."

Upon their arrival in Miami, the exiles were housed in temporary barracks near the airport nicknamed Casas de la Libertad (Houses of Liberty). Under a resettlement program established by the U.S. government, thousands went to live in states as far away as Alaska and Wyoming—in many ways, worlds removed

The Peter Pan Kids

Shortly after taking power, the Castro regime instituted programs in schools that would indoctrinate children with regime dogma and philosophy. A number of parents feared that they would lose their parental rights, and subsequently, their ties with their sons and daughters. They made a heartbreaking decision: to send the children unaccompanied to the United States to escape the Castro regime.

From late 1960 until 1962, some 14,000 Cuban youngsters were sent to the United States in what became known as Operation Peter Pan. The Catholic Archdiocese of Miami organized the operation, with help from Castro opponents in Cuba. The children first stayed in camps in South Florida; from there, some moved in with relatives. Others ended up with strangers who volunteered to take them in.

When the Cuban Missile Crisis of 1962 ended all flights from Cuba to the United States, Operation Peter Pan ended, too. For the kids who had made it to the United States, it was very difficult knowing they might not see their parents again. Most families eventually reunited, however. When the Freedom Flights began in December 1965, the parents of the Peter Pan children were given priority. Some 5,000 families were reunited within the first six months of the Freedom Flights.

from the Cuban neighborhoods of South Florida. But most found their way back to Miami or moved to Union City and West New York, towns in New Jersey that by that point had a large Cuban population.

In the 1960s, the attorney general's authority to "parole" people into the United States allowed Cubans to stay lawfully in the United States. However, granting parole status to Cubans did not guarantee permanent residence (the right to stay permanently). The Cuban Adjustment Act, passed in 1966, changed that. It allowed Cubans, regardless of how they arrived, to become permanent residents (green card holders) after being physically present in the United States for two years (later reduced to one year). The act conferred a unique privilege on Cuban migrants under U.S. law. Whereas undocumented (illegal) migrants from other countries are subject to detention and deportation, any Cuban reaching U.S. soil becomes eligible for permanent residency. Between 1946 and 2013, 2013, more than a million Cubans were granted permanent resident status.

President Lyndon B. Johnson signed the Cuban Adjustment Act while standing in front of the Statue of Liberty, a symbol of America's open policy toward immigrants and refugees. "I declare this afternoon to the people of Cuba that those who seek refuge here in America will find it," he said. "The dedication of America to our traditions as an asylum for the oppressed is going to be upheld."

The new law recognized the reality that most arriving Cubans were not going to live in the United States temporarily, as the Golden Exiles had believed they would upon their arrival in the early 1960s. The law was also a reminder to Cubans that seven years had passed since the Castro takeover, and that ousting him could not be accomplished as quickly as they once believed. Although many did not completely forget about organizing a resistance against the dictatorship, they did begin to focus more on resettling and rebuilding their lives and careers in their new land.

Mariel

Relatively few Cubans arrived in the first years after the Freedom Flights ended in 1973. In 1979, just 2,644 made their way to the United States, the fewest since the start of the revolution. But the following year, over 125,000 Cubans arrived in the space of just five months. This third major exodus was the Mariel boatlift, which was sparked by the actions of 12 Cubans from Havana. On April 1, 1980, the group commandeered a bus and crashed the gates of the Peruvian embassy, hoping to take advantage of a diplomatic custom that recognizes embassies as places of refuge for those fleeing repression.

When word got out that the group of 12 had successfully defected, thousands headed to the Peruvian embassy to seek asylum, too. Looking to dump the burden entirely on Peru, the Castro government removed its security detail, and soon 10,800 Cubans crowded the embassy compound. Peru granted all of them asylum, but then the Castro regime, embarrassed at the spectacle of so many citizens wanting to leave, sealed off the neighborhood and allowed no one to leave.

The embassy was, of course, not prepared to house, feed, and provide bathrooms for nearly 11,000 people. Conditions in the compound became terrible. People slept on the ground, went hungry, and lived in filth. Facing pressure from the international community and its own people, the Castro government finally decided to allow the people in the embassy to exit the country. What's more, it opened the port of Mariel to anyone who wanted to leave. As had happened after the opening of Camarioca 15 years earlier, thousands of Cubans took advantage of the opportunity.

However, the scale of the Mariel exodus was much bigger than that of the Camarioca boatlift. By the middle of May, 3,000 Cubans were arriving in South Florida every day. On the peak day, June 3, no less than 6,000 Cubans landed—a larger total than that of the entire Camarioca boatlift.

But the flood turned into a trickle in August when the U.S. Navy and Coast Guard began to turn back boats that were leav-

A boat full of Cuban refugees arrives in Key West, Florida, as part of the massive Mariel boatlift of 1980. The state government of Florida was challenged to handle the sudden influx of more than 125,000 refugees.

ing South Florida to pick up relatives in Mariel. All activity ended when the Cuban government shut down the port of Mariel on September 25. By that date, 125,266 Cubans had made it to freedom since the boatlift began.

The exiles of this third wave differed in many ways from those of previous waves. There were many more non-whites—estimated totals of this group in the boatlift range from 15 to 40 percent, at a time when perhaps 95 percent of Cubans in America were white. Also, a larger segment of this exile group were writers, musicians, painters, and other artists who no longer wanted to endure the restrictions on freedom of expression imposed in Cuba.

Most Marielitos were blue-collar workers, unlike the majority of the Golden Exiles, who were professionals. In this respect the Marielitos had more in common with the people who left on the Freedom Flights. Yet there was one important difference between the two groups: the exiles of the Freedom Flights included many people who had once owned small businesses and had entrepreneurial skills that they quickly put to use in the United States, while most Mariel refugees—a majority of whom were young men—had grown up under a communist economy that banned private businesses. Relatively few of them had entrepreneurial skills.

The Mariel boatlift was a tremendous shock to the state of Florida, as the Miami community suddenly had to deal with 125,000 new arrivals. It was faced with many new challenges: Where would the immigrants find housing and jobs? How could their school-age children, totaling more than 12,000, find room in local schools?

While the exodus increased the labor force in the Miami area by 7 percent over this short period, a January 1990 study in *Industrial and Labor Relations Review* by Princeton University economist David Card found that the Marielitos did not disrupt the city's labor market. "The Mariel immigration had essentially no effect on the wages or employment outcomes of non-Cuban workers in the Miami labor market," Card wrote. "And, perhaps even more surprising, the Mariel immigration had no strong effect on the wages of other Cubans." What Card observed, as many economists have also found, is that while immigrants fill jobs, they also create jobs through consumer spending, investment, and business start-ups.

At first, Mariel refugees were temporarily housed in emergency shelters such as churches and gymnasiums. When these buildings were filled, officials placed refugees in improvised places like Miami's Orange Bowl Stadium and established a gigantic "Tent City" under a highway overpass near the Little Havana neighborhood. Later the refugees were transferred to processing centers in Key West, Tamiami Park, Opa Locka, and the Krome Detention Center near the marshes of the Everglades. There the refugees were fingerprinted, photographed, given medical tests, and questioned to make certain they were not spies or criminals.

Immigration officials released those exiles with sponsors who guaranteed they would not become a public charge. Some 60,000 who did not find sponsors were sent to camps in four military bases: Eglin Air Force Base, in the Florida Panhandle; Fort Chaffee, Arkansas; Fort Indiantown Gap, Pennsylvania; and Fort McCoy, Wisconsin. The camps were beset by violence committed by some of the criminals Castro had let loose, as well as riots that broke out at the Chaffee and Indiantown bases.

Owing to Castro's willingness to get rid of certain undesirable elements in Cuba, a number of the arrivals were criminals and mental hospital patients. Cuban officials had opened some of the country's jails and mental hospitals and put the inmates onto the Mariel boats. A U.S. House Appropriations Committee report found that approximately 10 percent of the Mariel Cubans may have had a mental illness or criminal background that would have made them ineligible to enter the United States.

Eventually, many of the worst Cuban criminals ended up in prison. Those in the refugee camps with no criminal record were released. Within 10 years, the Mariel generation reached a level of success similar to that of earlier waves of Cubans and had become a part of the community in South Florida.

The Rafters

The next major wave of Cuban immigration to the United States was set off by yet another crisis. Just before dawn on July 3, 1994, the Cuban coast guard stopped an old tugboat, the *13 de Marzo*, that was carrying 72 Cuban exiles who hoped to make it to the United States. The boat was stopped at sea just 7 miles (11 km) from Havana.

The government vessels rammed the *13 de Marzo* to make it sink, then sprayed the deck with high-pressure water hoses that sent people overboard and ripped babies from their mothers' arms. A total of 41 people drowned. The survivors were arrested on charges of attempting to leave the country illegally.

The Castro government called it an accident, but many Cuban citizens rejected that explanation. (A report from the

Cuban American demonstrators protest the Clinton administration's response to the rafter crisis of 1994. For the first time since 1959, Cuban refugees picked up at sea were not immediately brought into the United States; they were instead detained at the U.S. Navy base at Guantánamo Bay, Cuba.

Inter-American Commission on Human Rights would later conclude that the Cuban government was, in fact, responsible for massacring passengers aboard the *13 de Marzo*.)

After the incident, dissenters in Cuba began wearing black armbands in mourning. Protests became louder in August 1994, when 30,000 people took to the streets of Havana in the largest anti-government demonstration since Castro took power. Scores of protesters were arrested.

Tensions between the government and the people remained high. By the late summer of 1994, in an attempt to rid Cuba of the protester element, Castro once again ordered security forces to allow people to leave. In just a few weeks, some 32,000 Cubans made it to the United States. People were so desperate to leave they used almost anything that could float—inner tubes from tires, pieces of Styrofoam, plywood planks. Out at sea, refugees suffered sunburn, exposure, and dehydration. Some

A History of Cuban Migration

experts estimate that thousands drowned during the trek.

A primary difference between the rafters (or *balseros*, as they were called in Spanish) and earlier Cuban refugees was that the majority of rafters were too young to remember life in Cuba before Castro. They were truly the children of the revolution, and they had left behind the only life they knew. Another major difference was in the way the U.S. government received this group. Fearing another Mariel crisis, the administration of President Bill Clinton ruled that the rafters would not be allowed to immediately enter the country. It was a landmark decision: for the first time since 1959, Cuban refugees were not permitted automatic entry to the United States.

The government did not send the rafters directly back to Cuba, however. Until a decision was made about how to handle the rafters, they would be held in a camp at Guantánamo, a naval base that the U.S. had controlled since 1902. Over the first few months about a third of the 30,000 rafters at Guantánamo were granted entry to the United States on a case-by-case basis.

Their arrival was not a shock for the South Florida community as Mariel had been. The total of 30,000 refugees for this exodus was much lower than the 125,000 of Mariel, and Miami was more prepared to receive refugees this time. The Cuban community was more politically influential, much wealthier, and more integrated with the Miami establishment than it had been in 1980. All these factors meant that newcomers could more easily find jobs, housing, and education. Civic organizations such as the Cuban American National Council set up schools for children who had difficulty making the transition. Another group, the Cuban American National Foundation, provided employment and temporary health insurance benefits to a number of the refugees.

On September 9, 1994, the United States and Cuba signed an agreement whereby the U.S. would take Cubans it interdicted at sea to a "safe haven" outside of the United States, rather than letting them onto the mainland as they had before. In return, Cuba would actively discourage its citizens from sailing to America. The U.S. government also agreed to admit through legal channels a minimum of 20,000 Cuban immigrants a year in addition to the immediate relatives of Cubans who had become U.S. citizens. The government implemented this commitment primarily through lotteries of eligible Cuban citizens who wish to migrate. (As of 2015, the last lottery application period had been in 1998, when more than half a million Cubans entered—a powerful reminder of the widespread discontent in Cuba.)

On May 2, 1995, the United States signed a second agreement with the Castro government that paved the way for the admission of more Cubans housed at Guantánamo. Following this agreement, the United States began sending additional Cubans interdicted at sea directly back to Cuba, rather than to a third country. In exchange, Cuba promised not to take retaliatory action against the returnees.

By the end of May, the remaining rafters had been given permission to finally enter America. The United States, as part of its agreement with Cuba, had made it an official policy to no longer grant automatic asylum to Cubans fleeing Castro. In what would become known as the "wet foot/dry foot" policy, rafters caught at sea by U.S. authorities were sent back to Cuba, but those who made it to the U.S. shore would be allowed to stay.

The immigration agreements between the U.S. and Cuban governments, and especially the implementation of the American wet foot/dry foot policy, may have reduced the number of Cubans trying to reach the United States by sea. But attempts to cross the Florida Straits never stopped completely. In fiscal year 2014, for example, the U.S. Coast Guard reported picking up slightly more than 2,000 would-be Cuban migrants at sea. An additional 2,000 rafters made it to dry land in 2014.

By that time, however, more Cubans were attempting to enter the United States by a different—and much longer—route. After the Castro regime's 2012 decision to end the requirement that citizens buy an exit permit to travel abroad, some Cubans began trying to get to the United States by first flying to a third country. Ecuador became the most popular destination because it doesn't require foreign travelers to get a visa.

From Ecuador, would-be migrants to the United States have to make their way north through Colombia, Central America, and Mexico before arriving at the U.S. southern border. The trip can be harrowing. A Cuban doctor interviewed for a 2015 *Los Angeles Times* story described how she had survived a kidnapping in Colombia. Thieves and drug gangs prey on migrants throughout Central America. Mexican police often demand bribes to allow Cubans to continue their journey north. "Lots of people die," a Cuban who had successfully made the trip from Ecuador told the *Los Angeles Times*. "We prefer to improve our lives and risk it. We arrived by the grace of God."

An estimated 44,000 Cubans reached the U.S. southern border in fiscal year 2015, up from about 17,500 the previous fiscal year. That increase, immigration analysts say, was driven by the announcement of normalized relations between the United States and Cuba. Many Cubans believed it was just a matter of time before the United States would end the preferential treatment Cuban undocumented immigrants received under the Cuban Adjustment Act. With difficult economic conditions and continuing political repression in their homeland, there was no shortage of Cubans willing to risk everything to start a new life in the United States while they still could.

Cubans in Canada

The historic ties between Canada and Cuba are weaker than those between the United States and Cuba, and as a result, Canada has not been a traditional destination for Cubans escaping either the Castro dictatorship or any of the repressive regimes that preceded it. Another decisive factor working against Cuban immigration to Canada is the great distance between the two countries. A boatlift from Cuba to Canada would be impractical; a "rafter" exodus, impossible.

Still, though their numbers are relatively low, some Cuban exiles have resettled in Canada. They enter the country in one of two ways—either as immigrants or as political refugees. Those entering as immigrants must meet the requirements of Canada's immigration laws, meaning they would likely have to qualify under the Canadian points system (which gives preference to immigrants with more education, work experience in certain fields, and English or French language skills) or be eligible for entry on humanitarian grounds.

Until relatively recently, Cubans had complained that legitimate asylum applicants were too often denied asylum and then deported. They argued that the Canadian government's friendly relations with the Castro regime kept immigration authorities from really seeing the persecution that Cubans faced. But there have been fewer complaints since the late 1990s. At that time, coinciding with a new Canadian foreign policy that was more openly critical of the Castro government, Canadian immigration authorities began to give more credibility to Cubans' fears of persecution. As a result, more defectors have been permitted to stay.

Over the years, small groups of visiting Cuban athletes and musicians have been granted asylum in Canada. One of the most well-known cases of group defection occurred in the summer of 2002, when 22 members of a Cuban Catholic youth group defected while in Toronto for a church service given by Pope John Paul II. They were sheltered in safe houses by the Cuban Canadian Foundation and eventually given asylum as political refugees.

 ## Text-Dependent Questions

1. Who are the "Golden Exiles"?
2. What incident triggered the Mariel boatlift?
3. Why has the normalization of U.S.-Cuba relations prompted an upswing in Cuban undocumented immigration to the United States?

 ## Research Project

Read about the history of Cuba. Create a timeline that includes the most important events, from the colonial era to the present.

A History of Cuban Migration

4 New American Lives

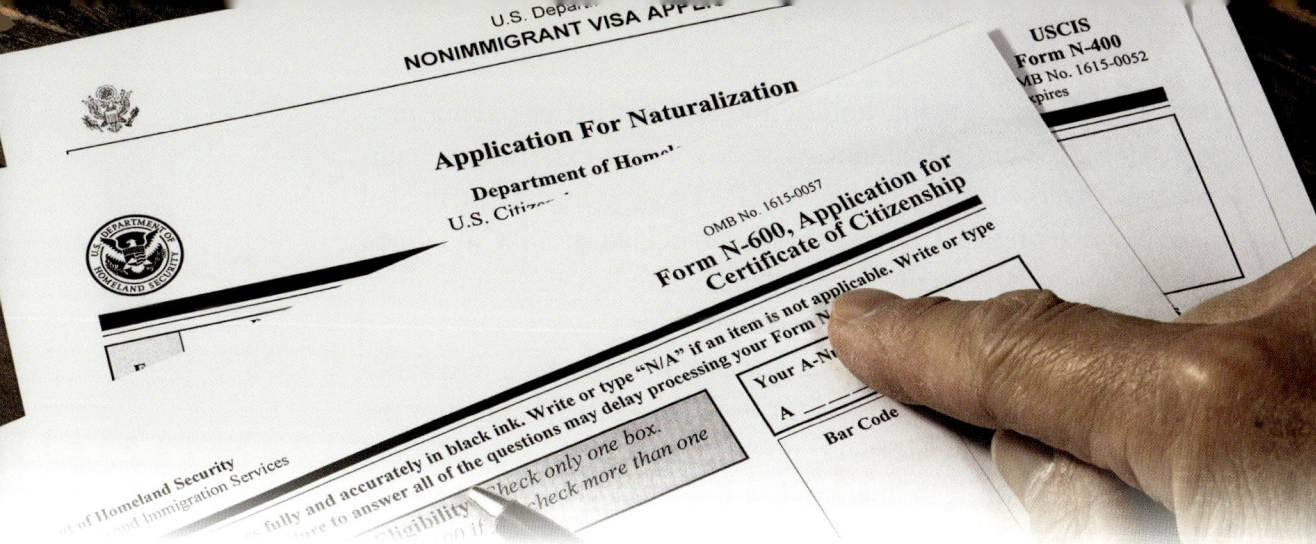

The first wave of Cubans to arrive in the United States after the 1959 revolution generally worried less about resettling than had the many millions of immigrants arriving before and after them. Unlike other immigrant groups, these Cuban exiles believed they would be living only temporarily in the United States. They planned to return to Cuba after the overthrow of Fidel Castro.

For these Cuban exiles, the failure of the Bay of Pigs invasion was hugely dispiriting. Smaller hit-and-run guerrilla operations continued after Bay of Pigs, though without the valued support of the United States. By the mid-1960s major developments had dashed the exiles' hopes that the Castro regime would soon fall. There was Castro's new alliance with the Soviet Union, which gave the regime support from a formidable superpower, and there was the prohibition of exile attacks launched from American soil, which grew out of the U.S.–Cuba agreement which followed the Cuban Missile Crisis. What allowed many Cubans to achieve permanent resettlement was the adoption of the Cuban Adjustment Act in 1966, which changed the legal status of exiles from temporary refugees to permanent residents.

Exiles still had dreams of returning to a free Cuba one day, but they began to realize it would take some time. They turned

◀Cuban Canadians cheer at a sporting event in Toronto. The Cuban community in Canada is considerably smaller than the one in the United States, largely due to the difficulty of Cuban migrants to reach the country compared to the US.

their attention to buying homes and seeking better-paying professional jobs, but it was not easy. Not every exile was a high-powered, well-educated professional. Those who had struggled to make a living in Cuba generally struggled at first in North America, too. And many did not speak English well enough to work in their professions in the United States.

In 1961 the federal government began to provide assistance with the Cuban Refugee Program. In its 20 years of existence the program would aid exiles with medical care, clothing, food, and social services—though many say it was more than paid back through the economic contributions of successful Cuban exiles.

The Boom of the Cuban American Community

The Cuban success story began in great part with small mom-and-pop shops. Homesick exiles wanted a taste of Cuba, whether it was a recording of Cuban-style son music or the down-home flavor of rice and beans. A handful of entrepreneurs set out to meet that demand. When they could not find American food distributors who carried yucca or malanga (tubers that are staples in the Cuban diet), they found out where that kind of produce was grown in Latin America and imported it. If mainstream supermarkets did not stock Cuban bread, they had Cuban bakers make it themselves.

Later, entrepreneurs extended their businesses beyond Cuban products and stores. They began to open flower shops, auto mechanic garages, furniture stores, and funeral parlors. By the middle of the decade, a neighborhood of southwest Miami became so Cubanized it became known as "Little Havana." It

 Words to Understand in This Chapter

capital—money or other assets that can be used to start or expand a business.
collateral—property used to secure a debt.
entrepreneur—a person who takes on the financial risks of organizing and operating a business.

Typical Cuban restaurant at SW Eighth Street, a focal point of the Cuban community in Miami. In the early 1960s, Cubans began opening up salons, shops, and restaurants all over the city's southwest section, which eventually became known as "Little Havana."

was filled with Cuban restaurants, bodegas, and other retail shops. In the professional community, Cuban doctors, pharmacists, accountants, dentists, and lawyers began to pass the tests that gave them the credentials to work in the United States.

As years passed, Cuban-owned businesses expanded. Owners of small bodegas turned their stores into supermarkets, which then became supermarket chains. Investors began to build small factories and buy real estate. Some who had been top banking executives in Cuba opened banks in Miami. These bankers played a key role in the Cuban community's growth.

Most businessmen had little capital to start or expand a business because the Castro government had taken their property and money when they left Cuba. As a result, they had little or no collateral with which to qualify for a new loan. But at a crucial point the Cuban bankers stepped in, offering what were called "character loans" to Cuban investors based on the bankers' personal knowledge of the applicants and their business know-how. This system saw great results in Miami, as the loans that were used to build businesses helped form the base of what is now the city's multibillion-dollar economy.

During that same period, similar developments were occurring in the New Jersey towns of Union City and West New York. Located in northern Hudson County, across the Hudson River from New York City, the region has been a magnet for newcomers since the middle of the 19th century. German immigrants first arrived there, followed by Irish and Italian immigrants in the early 1900s. A majority who settled there worked in the embroidery factories that dotted the two towns.

A Cuban-American waitress is ready to serve a meal at a restaurant in Union City, New Jersey.

A number of individuals from each immigrant group found economic success, and during the mid-1960s they left the gritty streets of Union City and West New York for the comforts and green lawns of the suburbs. During this mass relocation, Cubans began to flock to the area in large numbers.

The Italian American exodus left Bergenline Avenue, a main thoroughfare, virtually deserted. Stores were shuttered and windows were whitewashed, but Cuban immigrants soon arrived and brought the area back to life. They revived the district by opening stores that catered to the exiles, from Cuban sandwich shops to grocery stores to restaurants. By the late 1970s and early 1980s, the majority of stores on Bergenline Avenue were owned by Cubans.

With the large-scale development of the 1960s—the new Cuban shops, Cuban restaurants, Cuban professional services, and Spanish-language television and radio shows—immigrants could now immerse themselves almost entirely in Cuban culture. Cubans had great success in re-creating their homeland, not only in Miami, where the palm trees, the weather, and even the Spanish-style architecture were reminiscent of Cuba, but also in far-off New Jersey, with its cold winters and gray brick buildings that called up few memories of the Cuban landscape.

The One-and-a-Halfers

The generation that had brought families to the United States in the 1960s generally remained Cuban in cultural outlook. The transplanted communities they had created allowed them to preserve many facets of their lives in Cuba: they read Cuban newspapers, listened to Cuban radio stations, and ate at Cuban restaurants.

The Milkman Who Led the Way

It is not surprising that so many Cuban exiles ended up in Miami. After all, the city is located only 200 miles (322 km) from Cuba, and both places have similarly warm weather as well as tropical features like the majestic royal palm trees.

But how did 100,000 Cubans wind up in far-off North Hudson, in the towns of Union City and West New York? If some immigrants were willing to head north, why didn't they settle in New York City, which is better known as a historic exile destination? The answer to that question can be traced back to one immigrant couple from Fomento, a small town in the Las Villas province of central Cuba.

In 1949, newlyweds Manuel and Lydia Rodríguez spent their honeymoon in Miami Beach, where they befriended an Italian American woman. She lived in North Hudson but was spending the summer as a waitress in a local hotel. When the Rodríguezes' vacation ended, they did not go back to Cuba but instead drove north with their new American friend to North Hudson, where they decided to resettle.

Soon the Rodríguez couple opened their own milk delivery business. Friends from Fomento, impressed by the Rodríguezes' success, made their way to Union City, too. By the mid-1950s an estimated 2,000 to 3,000 Cubans lived in the area. It had become such a well-known destination that Fidel Castro visited it in 1955 during a fund-raising tour of Cuban communities in the United States.

The Cuban businesses and organizations established in the 1950s helped attract tens of thousands of exiles after Castro took power. Today there is still a Fomento Social Club right off the main shopping district, a reminder of the first Cubans who settled in the area more than six decades ago.

Freedom Tower in Miami was designed as a memorial to Cuban immigration. This Miami landmark was declared a U.S. National Historic Landmark in 2008.

But in the early 1970s, the situation began to change for the Cuban community in the United States. The children of the original exiles, who by this period were teenagers or college students, were becoming the first truly Cuban *American* generation. This group has been called "the one-and-a-halfers." (The parents, the original exiles, are "first generation" because they were the first to come to America. The children are not considered "second generation" because even if they spent most of their lives in the United States, they were born in Cuba.)

By definition, the one-and-a-halfers were situated somewhere between generations, the products of two cultures. Because they had grown up in Cuban neighborhoods, they learned Spanish and grew familiar with the food, music, and traditions of Cuban culture. But their neighborhoods were not completely beyond the influence of American culture. The one-and-a-halfers often spoke English better than Spanish, dressed in American-style clothes, and in some cases were as likely to eat a hamburger and fries from a fast-food chain as a traditional Cuban meal of *arroz con pollo* (chicken with rice).

The one-and-a-halfers who attended college began to graduate in the late 1970s and early 1980s, at a time when it was becoming clear that the elder generation had achieved remarkable success over a short time. Owing in great part to the hard work and dedication of that generation, by 1979 more than 60 percent of Cuban families owned their homes. In Miami, more than one-third of all businesses were Cuban-owned.

This next generation brought up in the United States followed in the footsteps of its elders. After facing the chaos of the Mariel crisis, and the challenges of helping to settle 125,000 fellow Cubans, the one-and-a-halfers continued to develop a Cuban American identity. Their unique perspective was shaped by their American schooling and experiences in the U.S. workplace. They became more knowledgeable about American

A Cuban American performs the drums on a street in Little Havana.

New American Lives

culture, and more comfortable in the wider English-speaking world outside their ethnic community.

One result of their efforts was the election of Cuban Americans to political office. During the 1980s, in Miami, the nearby city of Hialeah, and Union City, New Jersey, Cuban Americans were elected mayors. By the early 1990s, there were three Cuban Americans in Congress—Ileana Ros-Lehtinen and Lincoln Díaz-Balart, Republicans from South Florida, and Democrat Robert Menendez, from Union City. Díaz-Balart's brother, Mario, joined the group of representatives when he was elected in 2002. Other public figures of the one-and-a-half generation have led Cuban advocacy groups. One such individual is Jorge Mas, head of the Cuban American National Foundation (CANF) between 1981 and 1997. Considered the most influential anti-Castro group, CANF helped lobby for the U.S. trade embargo of Cuba, first implemented in 1960.

The Dialogue

One of the most controversial crises of Cuban exile history was El Diálogo (the Dialogue), which occurred in the late 1970s. The "dialogue" in this case was between Cuban exiles and the Castro government. After the 1959 revolution, exile leaders maintained a policy of opposing any negotiation with the regime. They believed that while talks would give the impression of improved relations, they would ultimately not promote democracy. But in 1977, a faction of exiles decided to disregard that policy. It initiated secret negotiations with the Cuban government, which agreed to release some political prisoners and, for the first time since Castro became president, allow exiles to visit the island. When the negotiations were made public, many exiles grew distressed by the news.

There were protest marches in Washington, D.C., and in the Cuban centers of Miami and North Hudson. Businesses that were owned by exiles involved in El Diálogo were boycotted. Travel agencies that organized trips to Cuba were bombed, and at least two prominent *dialogueros* were killed. A terrorist group that called itself Omega 7 took responsibility for the murders.

By the mid-1980s the FBI had caught and imprisoned most of the violent anti-Diálogo militants. The killings and bombings stopped, and so did El Diálogo. To some, the negotiations succeeded in that dozens of long-held political prisoners were released, and a number of exiles were able to visit relatives back in Cuba. However, others argued that El Diálogo did nothing to change the regime's unjust policies.

Pope Francis, the leader of the Roman Catholic Church, celebrates mass in Havana's Revolution Square during his 2015 visit to Cuba. A large proportion of Cuban Americans follow the Catholic religion.

The one-and-a-halfers have made contributions in many other ways. In Miami, they are among the city's leading political figures, business executives, academics, journalists, and artists.

Overall, the Golden Exiles and the one-and-a-halfers have attained impressive success in the United States, ranking at the

New American Lives 75

A group of young Cuban Americans enjoy the Miami beach. Children of the first waves of Cuban exiles are generally more Americanized than their parents and more comfortable in English-speaking environments beyond Little Havana and other Cuban neighborhoods.

top of Hispanic immigrant groups—and near the national averages—in a variety of economic and educational measures. Later arrivals have not been quite as successful—and as of 2013, according to the Pew Research Center, 56 percent of Cuban immigrants living in the United States had arrived since 1990.

A Growing Cuban Canadian Community

In 2011, the Canadian census recorded only 21,440 residents of Cuban ancestry. Not surprisingly, given their small numbers, the experience of Cuban Canadians differs markedly from the experience of Cuban Americans. There are no predominantly Cuban neighborhoods in Canada, not even in multicultural Toronto, the city with the largest number of Cuban residents. Consequently, there are few Cuban restaurants and clubs to remind newcomers of the tastes and sounds of home.

But Cuban immigrants in Canada would not appear to be in

any danger of losing their culture. From 2004 to 2013, Canada admitted a total of 11,641 Cubans as permanent residents. The Cuban Canadian community is young and growing—making it increasingly easy for the children of newcomers to grow up bicultural.

 Text-Dependent Questions

1. What is "Little Havana"?
2. Who are the "one-and-a-halfers"?
3. Which city is home to the largest Cuban community in Canada?

 Research Project

Choose a Cuban American or Cuban Canadian who has achieved success in business, politics, music, sports, or another field that interests you. Write a two-page biography.

5 OLD TRADITIONS LOST AND KEPT

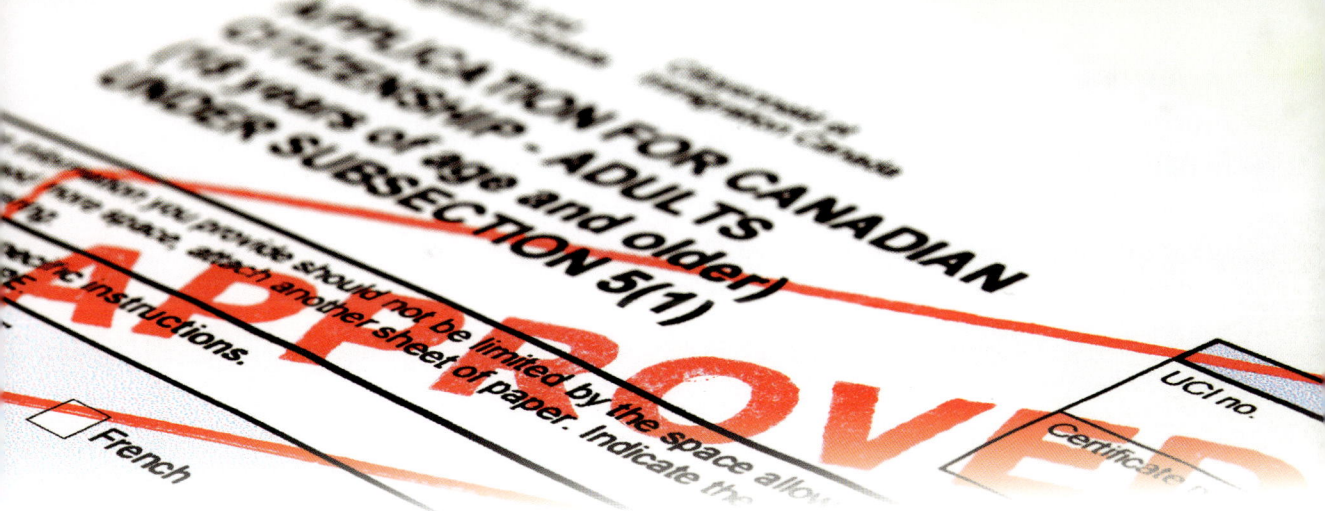

Like other people who left their country to settle in a new land, Cubans brought their nation's traditions to the United States. Some of those customs were lost, while others were kept and were even adopted by non-Cubans. Conversely, Cubans have also embraced several American traditions.

Traditions Lost

Old Cuba inherited from Spain the tradition of the siesta, a nap that is part of a long lunch break in the middle of the day. People would leave their workplaces in the afternoon and eat a long, leisurely *almuerzo*, a full-blown midday dinner. After the *almuerzo*, Cubans would take a nap before returning to work two or three hours later.

The rapid pace of life in the United States makes a siesta next to impossible. Whether Americans work in factories, offices, stores, or outdoors, they typically get one hour for lunch, sometimes less. So Cuban newcomers have had to adjust. Still, though the siesta is no more, some people, particularly elders, continue to have a large *almuerzo* in the afternoon instead of a light lunch. It often is the main meal of the day.

◂ Schoolchildren line up for a Three Kings Day Parade in New York City. The holiday, popular in Cuban communities, commemorates the three kings of the Gospels who brought frankincense, gold, and myrrh to the baby Jesus.

Another tradition that did not survive the migration to America completely intact is the Carnaval celebration, a festival popular in most Hispanic nations. The merrymaking of Carnaval takes place before the beginning of Lent, a religious season leading up to Easter for Catholics and members of other Christian denominations. (New Orleans' Mardi Gras is an American version of Carnaval). Cuba's Carnaval has parades with floats, masquerades, and dancing to conga and other forms of traditional music.

Although it's not really a Carnaval, the Festival de la Calle Ocho (Eighth Street Festival) is a popular festival among Cubans. Celebrated in March, the festival is named for the main thoroughfare of Miami's Little Havana. First held in 1978, it includes some Carnaval-like festivities such as floats, beauty pageants, and music; however, most of the action takes place on a stage rather than as a street parade, and the celebration also doesn't always coincide with Lent. Some of the most popular performers in the Spanish-speaking world have given concerts for this Miami festival, playing music from salsa to rock and pop *en español* (in Spanish). It may not be a Carnaval, exactly, but Festival de la Calle Ocho has become one of the largest celebrations of Hispanic culture in the United States, regularly attracting up to one million people.

One Cuban celebration that may be disappearing is El Día de los Tres Reyes Magos (Three Kings Day). In Spanish-speaking countries, the tradition was for children to receive gifts not on Christmas Day, and not from Santa Claus, but on Three Kings Day (January 6) from Melchor, Gaspar, and Baltasar—the Three

 Words to Understand in This Chapter

denomination—a large group of religious congregations united under a common faith.
pilgrimage—a journey to a sacred place.
siesta—an afternoon nap or rest, formerly common in many Hispanic countries.

Flag-waving teenagers watch the Cuban Day Parade in New York. Other patriotic Cuban celebrations include the birthday of revolutionary José Martí; Grito de Yara (Cry of Yara), which remembers the Ten Years War with Spain; and Grito de Baire (Cry of Baire), which remembers the beginning of the War of Independence in 1895.

Kings who, according to the Gospels, arrived in Bethlehem bringing gifts of frankincense, gold, and myrrh for the baby Jesus.

In North America, Cuban children typically get their gifts from Santa on Christmas. However, some families maintain the Three Kings tradition, and some communities even organize Tres Reyes Magos parades, with the Three Kings arriving on camels with sacks of toys.

Traditions Kept

The patriotic observances of Cuban history are, of course, not treated as official holidays in the United States and Canada, yet they continue to be observed in Cuban communities. These include January 28, the birthday of national hero José Martí in 1853; and February 24, Grito de Baire (Cry of Baire), marking the start of the War of Independence in 1895. Other important

Cuban Americans enjoy a parade in Miami Beach.

dates are May 20, commemorating Cuban Independence in 1902; October 10, Grito de Yara (Cry of Yara), which set off the Ten Years' War against colonial Spain (1868–78); and December 7, the Cuban equivalent of Memorial Day in the United States. This holiday marks the anniversary of the death of Antonio Maceo, one of the leading Cuban generals in the War of Independence who died in battle. The celebrations are usually marked with patriotic speeches and the singing of the Cuban and American national anthems.

There is also the anniversary of the Bay of Pigs invasion in mid-April. In Cuba, it is a triumphal celebration that marks the victory of Castro's army over the exiles of Brigade 2506. In America's Cuban communities, the perspective on the holiday is the exact opposite: veterans of Brigade 2506 hold somber observances to memorialize those who made the ultimate sacrifice in the invasion.

The Music of Cuba

One way Cubans in America keep their culture alive is through music. No cultural tradition of Cuba is more distinctive or more famous throughout the world than its music.

Like so many Cuban cultural forms, Cuban music started with a mixture of African and Spanish elements. Slaves would use boxes for drums and play the traditional rhythms of their African ancestors; musicians would play Spanish melodies on guitars and other stringed instruments over those rhythms, giving birth to what became Cuban music.

Cuban music has many styles, including *son, danzón, guajira*, mambo, and cha-cha. All of these styles are traditional, some more than a century old, yet they are alive and thriving in Cuban communities—in concerts, dance clubs, record shops, and on the radio. Cuban Americans listen to tunes sung by famous artists of the old days in Cuba, such as legendary singer Celia Cruz, or the more recent hits of Cuban American performers such as the Miami-born rapper Pitbull (Armando Christian Pérez).

There is also a recognizable Cuban influence in the world of jazz. Saxophonist Paquito D'Rivera and trumpet player Arturo Sandoval are two exiles whose combinations of Cuban rhythms with traditional jazz instrumentation have become known as "Latin jazz."

Cuba's National Pastime

Baseball is the national pastime not only of the United States, but also of Cuba. Because of the game's popularity in both countries, the love for the game has been one tradition Cubans have found easy to preserve as immigrants.

Baseball was introduced to Cuba in 1864, when three Cuban students from Alabama's Springhill College returned to Havana with baseballs and bats. Soon after, brothers Nemesio and Ernesto Guilló and their friend Enrique Porto founded the Habana baseball club. Ten years later a rival club, Almendares, was formed. Baseball soon became hugely popular, and a professional Cuban league began play in 1878.

Seven years before the Cuban league formed, Esteban Bellán became the Cuban to play in a U.S. league. Bellán was a shortstop for the Troy Haymakers, an old National Association team based in New York State. In 1911 Armando Marsans and Rafael Almeida joined the Cincinnati Reds as the first Cubans of the modern era to play major league baseball.

By the 1960s more than 100 Cubans had played in the American major leagues. Some of them were among the best players of their time, like pitchers Luis Tiant and Mike Cuellar, Minnesota Twins outfielder Tony Oliva (the only player to win batting titles in his first two major league seasons), and Cincinnati infielder Tony Pérez, the first Cuban player inducted into the Hall of Fame.

In the late 1960s the Castro regime severely curtailed the flow of players from Cuba to the majors. However, the number of Cubans increased again in the 1990s. At first, this new wave was made up of Cubans raised in the United States, such as José Canseco and Rafael Palmeiro. Later in the decade, players who had become stars in Cuba defected and joined major league teams, including Yankee pitcher Orlando Hernández and his brother Liván, also a pitcher. Players such as Yasiel Puig have continued this distinguished tradition. Puig, a slugger for the Los Angeles Dodgers, made his American debut in 2013.

Since entering the major leagues in 2012, New York Mets outfielder Yoenis Cespedes has become one of the game's most feared sluggers.

One religious holiday that Catholic Cuban Americans continue to maintain is September 8, La Virgen de la Caridad (Our Lady of Charity), commemorating Cuba's patron saint. It marks the day in the 1500s when, according to tradition, three fishermen in a small boat witnessed a miracle. They were about to be capsized in a tempest when they spotted a statue of the Virgin Mary floating in the storm-tossed waves, whereupon the storm immediately passed, and their lives were saved.

What many believe to be the original Virgin Mary statue can be found in a church in the Cuban town of El Cobre, near the city of Santiago. It is the destination of a pilgrimage held on September 8. Cuban communities in the United States observe the feast with a Catholic mass followed by a procession led by a statue of the Virgin. The largest and best known of these is held at the Hermita de la Caridad del Cobre, a Miami chapel that rests along Biscayne Bay. It has become the spiritual center of Cuban Catholics living in the United States.

The holiday of Christmas is, of course, observed in Cuban American communities, but not exactly in the fashion other Americans celebrate it. The most obvious difference is that the traditional meal is held on December 24, Christmas Eve, and not on Christmas Day itself. The food is distinctively Cuban, too. Families eat black beans with rice; boiled *yucca* in a Cuban sauce of garlic, olive oil, and lime juice; and roast pork marinated in garlic and spices such as cumin, oregano, and juice from special sour oranges. In places where the December weather is warm, such as Miami, the pig is roasted over a spit on an open fire. In colder American cities, Cubans follow the same recipe but roast the pig—or more likely a leg of pork—in the kitchen oven. For dessert, people eat *turrón*, a nut and honey bar that was first eaten in Spain and has been enjoyed for centuries.

Some Cuban traditions have been embraced by non-Cubans, especially in Miami, where eating a Cuban sandwich (ham, roast pork, and cheese on grilled Cuban bread) is about as common as eating a slice of pizza. Similarly, Miamians of all ethnic groups were used to drinking little cups of strong Cuban espresso long

Rooster sculpture with the colors of the Cuban and American flags at Calle Ocho, the focal point of the cuban community in Little Havana. The rooster is an important symbol in Cuban culture, representing strength and power.

before espresso bars became commonplace in the rest of the country.

New Traditions

Cubans in the United States don't only enjoy the traditions and festivities they brought from their old country; they have also adopted American holidays, often giving them a Cuban twist. For instance, Cuban American families celebrate Thanksgiving even though the holiday is unknown in Cuba. As in other American homes, Cuban families gather around the table to give thanks and eat turkey. But the turkey is prepared Cuban style (in much the same way as the Christmas roast pork) and is often stuffed with rice and black beans.

Fourth of July picnics are also popular. The younger kids may eat hot dogs and hamburgers, just like in a typical American celebration, but there may also be Cuban dishes such as *congrí* (rice and red beans cooked together with spices) and *chorizo*, a sausage Cubans adopted from the Spanish.

Text-Dependent Questions

1. Name the Cuban poet and patriot whose birthday Cuban Americans celebrate on January 28.
2. What are son, danzón, and guajira?
3. Which sport is Cuba's national pastime?

Research Project

To become a U.S. citizen, an immigrant from another country must pass a civics test. U.S. Citizenship and Immigration Services offers practice tests at: https://my.uscis.gov/prep/test/civics/view
    Take a test. What percentage did you get correct? Do some further research about any answers you got wrong.

Old Traditions Lost and Kept

6 A Community's Challenges

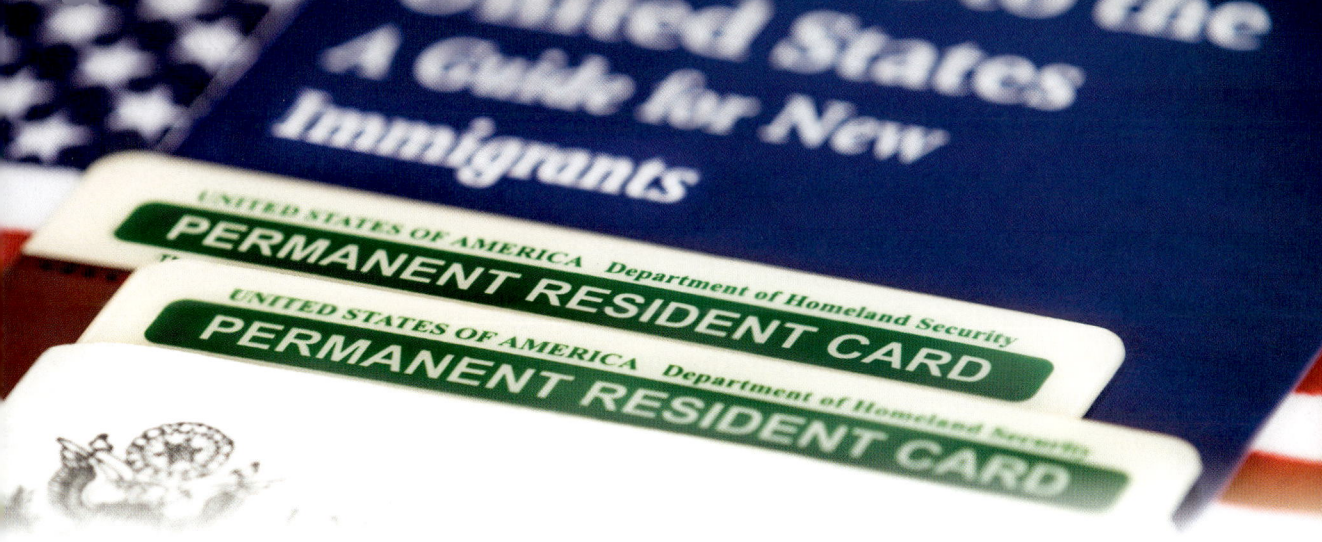

In 2010, according to data from the U.S. census, 29 percent of adult Cuban Americans had only a high school degree, which was almost identical to the percentage for the U.S. population as a whole (28 percent). The proportion of Cubans with a college degree was a bit below the national average (24 percent versus 28 percent), though among major Hispanic groups in the United States only Colombians and Peruvians ranked higher in that measure of educational attainment. At $40,000, Cuban Americans' median household income was also the median for Hispanic groups, but nearly $10,000 below median household income for the country overall.

If the Cuban American community has become thoroughly woven into the fabric of the United States, it also has some unique problems to overcome. These include persistent Cuban stereotypes as well as debates over immigration policy and bilingual government and education.

Language

In many American cities, speaking Spanish on a regular basis sometimes causes friction between Hispanics and their non-Hispanic neighbors, and Miami is no exception. There, because the Cuban community is so influential, Spanish is not restricted

◀ Many Cuban families who have settled in U.S. cities and suburbs still face serious issues, including the continuing debates over bilingual education, immigration policy, and negative portrayals of Cubans in the media.

to a particular neighborhood or group of people. It can be heard everywhere, from the most run-down neighborhoods to the most exclusive clubs and restaurants. Among the older generation of business leaders, it remains the language of choice.

By the 1970s, there were so many Spanish-speaking Cubans in South Florida that Dade County, which included Miami, passed a law in 1973 making its government officially bilingual. (The name of the county was officially changed to Miami-Dade County in 1997.) Legal documents, voting ballots, and notices to citizens were all made available in both English and Spanish. Many Miamians who did not know Spanish opposed this law and overturned it in a referendum in November 1980. At that time the community was reeling from the sudden influx of 125,000 Cubans who arrived during the Mariel crisis. County government returned to conducting business in English only.

However, little changed in the everyday communication of Dade County residents. People continued to speak the language of their choice, which was Spanish for hundreds of thousands of older Cubans. In 1993, a new generation of Cuban Americans comfortable with both languages successfully pushed to make Dade officially bilingual again.

Tensions still remain between non-Hispanics and Hispanics. Some non-Hispanics believe speaking Spanish in front of people who do not know the language is inappropriate. They also fear that the United States could fragment culturally without the English language as a unifying element for all citizens. The coun-

Words to Understand in This Chapter

indentured servant—a person who is obligated to work for another person (often without pay) in order to repay the costs of the journey to a new country.
refugee—a person who has been forced to leave his or country in order to escape war, persecution, or natural disaster.
triad—a secret society originating in China that is usually involved in organized crime.

90 Cuban Immigrants

terargument of Cubans, as well as other Hispanics in Miami, is that speaking Spanish should not be considered anti-American. The Spanish language is, after all, an outgrowth of their immigrant heritage, which they are entitled to keep as Americans.

Another major language issue is the debate over the best approach to teaching English to Cuban children, a particularly hot topic in South Florida school districts. Some educators favor bilingual education, a method under which children attend English classes designed for those learning a new language and take other subjects such as history or math in their native tongue. Then, when the students know English well enough, they switch over to regular classes taught in English. The intention of bilingual education is to prevent students from falling behind in subject areas such as math, science, and history while they are learning English.

But some educators are opposed to bilingual education, asserting that it does a poor job of teaching English and does not take advantage of young people's ability to easily pick up a new language. They also argue that many students never really learn English well enough to assimilate completely. As an alternative to bilingual education, they propose the English immersion system, under which students undergo intensive English-language courses for one or two years, and take their other subjects in English with students who already know English.

Yet a third system that educators have championed is called "dual immersion." In schools using this program, all students—whether they primarily speak English, Spanish, or another language—attend classes in English for one-half of the day, and then classes in another language for the day's other half. The goal is for everybody to learn two languages. Surprisingly, many on both sides of the bilingual education debate support dual immersion, though few schools offer the program.

In Miami, where most newly arrived Cuban children live, many schools offer bilingual programs. However, other communities favor immersion. The controversy is likely to continue in the years ahead.

Immigration

For decades, Cubans arriving in the United States have benefited from special considerations not given to other immigrants. From the very beginning of the Castro revolution, undocumented Cuban immigrants have been permitted to stay in the United States. Unless they're criminals, they're essentially guaranteed permanent residency (including the right to hold a job) and eventual U.S. citizenship.

By contrast, undocumented immigrants from other countries are subject to arrest and deportation. They cannot legally work in the United States, and they are ineligible for permanent resident status.

In the 1960s, when the U.S. policy of treating Cuban immigrants differently was instituted, the rationale seemed compelling. Those who sought to escape Cuba were very likely fleeing political repression, and undocumented migrants returned to the island would almost certainly have faced retribution from the Castro regime. Over time, however, it became clear that economics rather than political repression was driving most unauthorized immigration from Cuba. And today it would be hard to argue that undocumented migrants returned to Cuba would face greater danger than, say, undocumented migrants from Central America, whom the United States routinely deports.

Critics charge that the continued preferential treatment of Cuban undocumented immigrants reflects political considerations rather than any legitimate policy concern. Congress, they say, has simply been unwilling to risk political fallout from the Cuban American community, which might occur if the key provisions of the Cuban Adjustment Act were eliminated.

Stereotypes

Cuban Americans often complain that they are portrayed negatively on television and in newspapers. Some say that they are depicted as relentless lobbyists who take advantage of their political clout to put pressure on Cuba's communist government. The stereotype was raised more frequently during the crisis of

The story of six-year-old Elián González captured the interest of millions of Cubans and Americans. After a seven-month standoff, the Cuban boy was refused refugee status and returned to Cuba at his father's request.

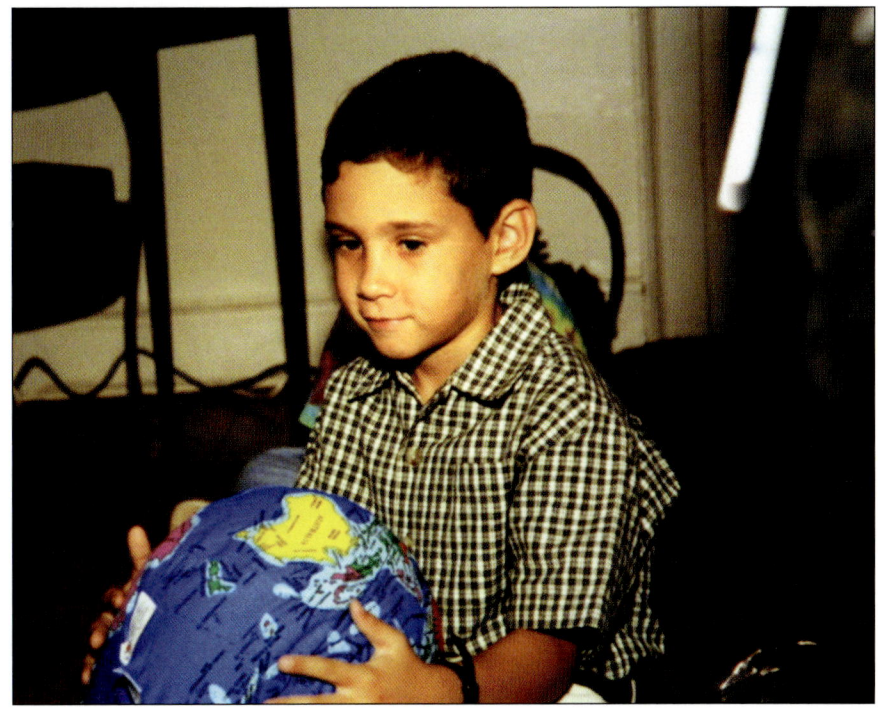

six-year-old Elián González, which began in late 1999 and ended in June 2000. Elián and his mother, Elisabet, attempted to flee to the United States on a small boat. She drowned during the journey, but Elián was rescued and turned over to an uncle who lived in Miami. Then Elián's father, Juan Miguel González, who was divorced from Elián's mother but kept in touch with the boy, asked for his son to be sent back to Cuba. The Miami relatives, fearing that González was asking for the return of his son under pressure from the Castro regime, insisted that González had to personally come to get Elián in order for them to release him.

The drama of the little boy soon became the subject of a national obsession, covered by 24-hour cable-television news programs and major newspapers. The standoff between Elián's father and his relatives went on for months. Then, to the surprise of most exiles, Juan Miguel González came to the United States to demand the return of Elián. In the meantime, thousands of Cuban Americans had gathered around the Little Havana home of Elián's relatives to support them.

Cuban Americans demonstrate outside the home of Elián González' relatives in Miami, April 2000. Thousands of Cuban Americans in Miami and other communities supported Elián's relatives in their fight to let the boy remain in the United States.

To nearly every Cuban American, it was a heartrending conflict. Escaping Cuba and finding freedom in the United States was a sensitive issue to all Cuban exiles. What made the story even more compelling for those supporting Elián's relatives was the idea that the boy's mother had given her life so that he could live in America. It seemed inconceivable to many Cuban Americans that the very country that had provided that freedom would send the boy back to a father who—some believed—was indoctrinated or pressured by the Castro government. A number of Americans and, eventually, the Clinton administration, viewed it differently: the boy's father wanted him back, and as a matter of law Elián belonged with him. In offices, in factories, and in just about every place of work in Miami, Cuban Americans and others argued about what to do with Elián.

The standoff ended in April 2000, when armed federal agents stormed the house where Elián was staying and gave the boy back to his father. Shortly after, the Elián ordeal was over, but not the trauma it caused among Cuban Americans. Community and civic leaders feared that the image the rest of the country had of Cubans had been seriously harmed. They started publicity campaigns to present a better image of Cuban immigrants and the anti-Castro cause.

But Americans' views of Cuba have shifted dramatically in recent years. In opinion polling conducted by the Gallup Organization in 2015, the percentage of Americans who viewed Cuba favorably nearly equaled the percentage who viewed Cuba unfavorably (46 percent versus 48 percent). Just nine year earlier, in 2006, Gallup had found 71 percent of Americans holding a negative view of Cuba, and just 21 percent holding a positive view. By a solid majority (59 percent to 30 percent), the 2015 Gallup poll found Americans in favor of reestablishing diplomatic ties with Cuba. Other polls showed that even among Cuban Americans, a majority favored normalized relations with Cuba.

Will these shifts herald changes to U.S. immigration policy regarding Cuba? That is a distinct possibility. In fact, a few members of Congress have made the once-unthinkable suggestion that Cuban undocumented immigrants not automatically be granted permanent residency. "The Cuban policy should be changed," Representative Henry Cuellar, a Texas Democrat, said in late 2015. "If we do that for them, why not do it for the Central Americans, the Mexicans, and for everyone else?"

Text-Dependent Questions

1. What change did Florida's Dade County (today called Miami-Dade County) make in 1973, reverse in 1980, and reinstitute in 1993?
2. According to 2015 opinion polls, did most Americans favor or oppose the normalization of U.S.-Cuba relations?

Research Project

The plight of six-year-old Elián González riveted the nation in late 1999 and early 2000. Find out where Elián is and what his life is like today. Has he said anything about his brief time in the United States?

7 THE FUTURE OF CUBAN IMMIGRATION

In 2013 Raúl Castro promised to step down in five years. If he keeps that pledge and leaves office in 2018, what will happen then? Will the same repressive system continue under different leaders? Or will there be a rebirth of democracy? Regardless of the final outcome, Cuban Americans will certainly be involved in shaping the island's future, even if the majority of them continue living in the United States.

Had the Castro government fallen in the 1960s or even in the 1970s, a large segment of the Cuban exile community would probably have gone back to Cuba. During those years just about every immigrant family had a desire to return. But attitudes have changed. Today, despite their longing for their homeland, most Cubans would probably remain in the United States even if democracy came to Cuba.

Despite the intentions of many Cuban Americans to remain in the United States, their ties with Cuba will undoubtedly remain strong. They may even have the opportunity to use the expertise they have gained in the United States to help rebuild Cuba in the post-Castro era. While living in the United States they have learned how democracy works from the inside; some have learned first-hand how to create a successful business. If

◀ US president Barack Obama talks on the phone with President Raúl Castro of Cuba in the Oval Office, December 16, 2014. The next day, President Obama announced that the United States would restore full relations with Cuba after more than 50 years.

the opportunity presented itself, they could perhaps play a role in promoting fair, open national elections after the communist regime is gone. Cuban business leaders could help rebuild the island's economy. However, one foreseeable problem of such efforts might be the resentment some native Cubans could feel toward the exiles. They could object to the idea of "Americanized" Cubans telling them what to do.

Politics

For decades, Cuban Americans were strong supporters of the Republican Party. That trend dated back to the defeat of the exiles at the Bay of Pigs, which many Cubans blamed on the decision of President Kennedy, a Democrat, not to provide American air support as the invasion foundered. After that, many Cuban Americans perceived Democratic policy as "soft" on Fidel Castro's regime.

According to exit polls, more than 80 percent of Cuban Americans voted for Republican presidential candidates Ronald Reagan and George H. W. Bush. Support for Republicans slipped in the 1996 election, during a time when some felt that the party supported anti-Hispanic, anti-immigrant policies.

Yet Republican Bob Dole still won about 6 in 10 votes cast by Cuban Americans in 1996. In 2000, Republican George W. Bush captured three-quarters of the Cuban American vote, which helped him win Florida and, ultimately, the presidency.

But the Republican Party can no longer count on a big

 Words to Understand in This Chapter

exit poll—a poll taken of a sample of voters right after they've cast their ballots, used to predict election outcomes, determine the reasons for voting decisions, describe the demographic composition of the electorate, and collect other information.
expertise—great skill or knowledge in a particular field.
incumbent—a person currently holding an elected office.

advantage among Cuban American voters—or indeed, on any advantage at all. In 2012, Democrat Barack Obama, the incumbent president, bested Republican Mitt Romney by about 2 percentage points among Cuban Americans. Younger members of that community, as well as recent arrivals to the United States, tend to identify with the more liberal views of the Democratic Party. And with opinion polls showing a majority of Cuban Americans approving of the normalization of relations with Cuba, it's not at all clear that the charge Democrats are "soft" on the Cuban regime resonates anymore.

Politically, the Cuban American community is less unified today than it was in the past. But that's at least partly a measure of how successfully Cubans have assimilated in the United States. The 2016 presidential race offered a remarkable illustration of that success: two second-generation Cuban Americans, Senator Marco Rubio of Florida and Senator Ted Cruz of Texas, were leading contenders for the Republican Party's nomination.

The Youngest Cuban Americans

Nearly six decades have passed since the first Cuban exodus began. The original generation of exiles has grown old; some individuals have watched their friends die without seeing Cuba again. Many of the exiles' sons and daughters—the first truly bicultural and bilingual generation—have become well established in their jobs, and have had children of their own. These children—babies, grammar school kids, teenagers—are the newest generation of Cuban Americans. Their grandparents remained wholly Cuban; many of their parents have only dim memories of Cuba, as they were very young when they left. Members of this third generation, who only know life in the United States, will play a decisive role in shaping the future of Cuban immigration.

Many Cuban American children who live outside Miami and other cities heavily populated by Cubans are enjoying a high level of assimilation in schools with few other Cuban or Hispanic kids. At home these children may have Cuban meals,

Cuban-American Marco Rubio won one of Florida's two seats in the US Senate in 2010. He was an unsuccessful Republican candidate for president of the United States in the 2016 presidential primaries.

but beyond what they eat they may have few traits distinguishing them from other minority groups. They and their children several decades from now could perhaps be challenged to keep Cuban culture alive.

Even in Miami, a town soaked in Cuban atmosphere where Spanish can be heard everywhere, English is more often than not the youngest generation's language of choice. Cuban grandparents, who may not speak much English, sometimes have trouble communicating with their grandchildren.

Yet as the Cuban American community faces Americanization through its younger generation, another group, the newcomers, promises to preserve Cuban culture. This group includes the increasing numbers who have traveled overland to reach the U.S. southern border. The group's members may be adults, teenagers, or young children; all prefer speaking Spanish and are more thoroughly Cuban. Their presence in the Cuban communities of the United States will ensure that the immigrant population remains diverse in the years ahead.

In Canada, the relatively new Cuban community is just beginning a similar transformation. It will never be large enough to shape Canadian culture, politics, and economics in the manner that the 2 million Cuban Americans have done in the United States. Nonetheless, if the success of bicultural Cuban Americans is an indicator of what is possible in another country, there will eventually be a generation of successful, bicultural Cuban Canadians.

Until the day when the Cuban government implements radical changes, or the communist system collapses altogether, Cubans will continue a tradition now nearly 200 years old—dating back to the colonial struggle against Spain—of seeking the freedom in the United States and Canada they cannot find at home.

Text-Dependent Questions

1. What promise did Cuban leader Raúl Castro make in 2013?
2. Identify one reason most Cuban Americans supported the Republican Party from the early 1960s through the first decade of the 21st century.
3. Which Democratic presidential candidate won a majority of the Cuban American vote, and in what year?

Research Project

President Obama's decision to restore diplomatic relations with Cuba was praised by some American leaders and criticized by others. Find three arguments for, and three arguments against, the normalization of U.S.-Cuba relations. Then write a short essay explaining which side you agree with and why.

Famous Cuban Americans

Desi Arnaz (1917–86), costar with wife Lucille Ball of the hugely popular 1950s TV sitcom *I Love Lucy*. Arnaz was also a producer and director, and was the first to use a three-camera studio setup, a practice that became standard in television production.

Jeffrey Preston "Jeff" Bezos (1964–), a technology entrepreneur and investor who founded online retail giant Amazon.com in 1994.

Celia Cruz (1925–2003), veteran salsa singer who first became a star in Cuba in the 1950s and later sought exile in the United States, where she continued her career.

Rafael Edward "Ted" Cruz (1970–), U.S. senator from Texas and 2016 presidential candidate who was born in Calgary, Alberta, Canada.

Cameron Michelle Díaz (1972–), a Hollywood actress most famous for her roles in the Charlie's Angels and Shrek series of films. She is one of the highest-paid actresses in Hollywood.

Gloria Estefan (1958–), Grammy-winning singer who, along with her husband and record producer Emilio Estefan, combined Cuban rhythms with American pop melodies to sell more than 70 million albums worldwide. She has recorded albums in Spanish as well as in English.

Andy García (1956–), critically acclaimed actor, known for his performances in *The Untouchables*, *Internal Affairs*, and *The Godfather: Part III*, for which he received an Oscar nomination.

Roberto Goizueta (1931–97), former chief executive officer of the Coca-Cola Company and one of the most admired executives in the business world. During his tenure as Coca-Cola's chief, which began in 1981, he raised the company's market value by 3,500 percent.

Oscar Hijuelos (1951–), author who won the Pulitzer Prize in 1989 for *The Mambo Kings Play Songs of Love*. The novel, which was adapted into a movie in 1992, tells the story of Cuban musicians in New York in the early 1950s, when Latin music became popular in the United States.

Jorge Mas Canosa (1939–97), chairman of the Cuban American National Foundation who became hugely influential in helping to shape U.S. policy regarding the Castro regime.

Atanasio ("Tony") Pérez (1941–), first Cuban major-league baseball player inducted into the National Baseball Hall of Fame. In his career that spanned from 1964 to 1986, he hit 379 home runs and had 1,652 runs batted in.

Armando "Pitbull" Cristian Pérez (1981–), rapper from Miami whose hits include "Give Me Everything" and "Timber."

Ileana Ros-Lehtinen (1952–), Republican congresswoman and chair of the Subcommittee on International Operations and Human Rights. In 1989 she became the first Cuban American elected to the U.S. Congress.

Marco Rubio (1971–), U.S. senator from Florida and 2016 presidential candidate.

Series Glossary of Key Terms

assimilate—to adopt the ways of another culture; to fully become part of a different country or society.

census—an official count of a country's population.

deport—to forcibly remove someone from a country, usually back to his or her native land.

green card—a document that denotes lawful permanent resident status in the United States.

migrant laborer—an agricultural worker who travels from region to region, taking on short-term jobs.

naturalization—the act of granting a foreign-born person citizenship.

passport—a paper or book that identifies the holder as the citizen of a country; usually required for traveling to or through other foreign lands.

undocumented immigrant—a person who enters a country without official authorization; sometimes referred to as an "illegal immigrant."

visa—official authorization that permits arrival at a port of entry but does not guarantee admission into the United States.

Further Reading

Antón, Alex, and Roger E. Hernández. *Cubans in America*. New York: Kensington Books, 2002.

Bourke, Dale Hanson. *Immigration: Tough Questions, Direct Answers*. Downers Grove, IL: InterVarsity Press, 2014.

Chomsky, Aviva. *Undocumented: How Immigration Became Illegal*. Boston: Beacon Press, 2014.

Gjelten, Tom. *A Nation of Nations: A Great American Immigration Story*. New York: Simon and Schuster, 2015.

Frank, Marc. *Cuban Revelations: Behind the Scenes in Havana*. Gainesville: University Press of Florida, 2013.

Merino, Noel. *Illegal Immigration*. San Diego: Greenhaven Press, 2015.

Mesa-Lago, Carmelo, and Jorge Pérez-López. *Cuba Under Raúl Castro: Assessing the Reforms*. Boulder, Colo.: Lynne Rienner Publishers, 2013.

Veciana-Suárez, Ana. *Flight to Freedom*. London: Orchard Books, 2002.

Internet Resources

www.lanuevacuba.com/megalinks.htm
A site with a comprehensive list of links to Cuban American sites.

www.miami.edu/iccas/iccas.htm
The University of Miami's Institute for Cuban and Cuban-American Studies serves as a resource center for those doing research on Cuban Americans and other related topics.

www.cuban-exile.com
The Cuban Information Archives is a fascinating collection of primary source materials pertaining to anti-Castro Cuban exile activities and developments.

www.cubagenweb.org/index.htm
A site entailing genealogical resources for those looking for their Cuban and Spanish roots.

www.cia.gov/library/publications/the-world-factbook/geos/cu.html
The CIA World Factbook Cuba page includes a wealth of data.

Publisher's Note: The websites listed on this page were active at the time of publication. The publisher is not responsible for websites that have changed their address or discontinued operation since the date of publication. The publisher reviews and updates the websites each time the book is reprinted.

Index

13 de Marzo, 64
   See also "rafter" crisis
1976 Immigration Act (Canada), 47
1952 Immigration and Nationality Act, 39–40
1965 Immigration and Nationality Act, 40–41

Almeida, Rafael, 86
Americas Watch, 32
Amnesty International, 32
Angola, 31
Arnaz, Desi, 102
Ashcroft, John, 60

baseball, 86
   See also culture
Batista, Fulgencio, **21**, 24–26, 52, **54**
Bay of Pigs invasion, 28, **29**, 56, 71, 84, 98
   See also exiles (Cuban)
Bellán, Esteban, 86
Berroa, Esteban, 48
Brigade 2506. *See* Bay of Pigs invasion
Brothers to the Rescue, 34
Bureau of Citizenship and Immigration Services (BCIS), 42
Bureau of Customs and Border Protection (BCBP), 42
Bureau of Immigration and Customs Enforcement (BICE), 42
Bush, George H. W., 98
Bush, George W., 17, 28, **43**, 60, **97**, 98–99
businesses (Cuban), 73–75
   See also Cuban Americans

de Cagigal, Juan Manuel, 48–49
Camagüey, Cuba, **21**
Camarioca, Cuba, 57
   See also exiles (Cuban)
Canada, 68–69, 79, **99**
   and Cuba, 27–28, 35, 69
   Cuban population in, 15, 69, 101
   immigration history, 45–47
Canosa, Jorge Mas. *See* Mas Canosa, Jorge
Canseco, José, 86
Carbonell, Nestor, 55–56
Card, David, 62–63
Carnaval celebration, 81–82
   See also culture
Casas de la Libertad (Houses of Liberty), 58
   See also exiles (Cuban)
Castro, Fidel, 15, 21, 48, 63, 75, 76, 91, 92
   dictatorship of, 26–35, 52–57, 58, 59, 60–61, 64–65, 71, 97–98
   and overthrow of Batista, 25–26
Castro, Raúl, 25
Chinese Exclusion Act of 1882, 37
   See also ethnicity
Clinton, Bill, 65, 99
communism, **26**, 27, 28, 30–31, 32–33
   See also Castro, Fidel
communities, 50–51, 58, 66, 73–78, 79, 100–101
Cruz, Celia, 85, 102
Cuba, 15, **17**, 18
   as colony of Spain, 21–23, 48–51, 53
   economy, 24, 31, 33–34
   under Fidel Castro, 26–35, 52–57, 58, 59, 60–61, 64–65, 71, 97–98
   flag, **50**
   under Fulgencio Batista, 24–26, 52
   and United States, 21, 23–24, 27–30, 31–34, 48–52, 56, 66–67
Cuban Adjustment Act (1966), 59, 71, 91
   See also refugees
Cuban American National Council, 66
Cuban American National Foundation, 66, 78, 102
Cuban Americans, 18–19, 100–101
   education, 89–91
   employment, 16, 73–75
   "one-and-a-halfers," 76–79

Numbers in ***bold italic*** refer to captions.

political involvement of, 17–18, 77–78, 97–100
population, 15, 47–48, **72**
socioeconomic status, 16–17
stereotypes, 92–95
Cuban Canadian Foundation, 69
Cuban Day Parade, **71**, **82**
See also holidays
Cuban Missile Crisis, 29–30, 56, 58, 71
See also Bay of Pigs invasion
Cuban Refugee Program, 72
See also refugees
Cuban Revolution, 25–26, 28, **29**, 55, 71
See also Castro, Fidel
Cuellar, Mike, 86
culture, 19, 75–77, 81–87, 101

Daza, Ignacio, 48
DeGrasse (Admiral), 48–49
Department of Homeland Security, 42
See also Immigration and Naturalization Service (INS)
El Día de los Tres Reyes Magos (Three Kings Day), **81**, 83
See also holidays
El Diálogo (the Dialogue), 76
See also exiles (Cuban)
Díaz-Balart, Lincoln, 78
Díaz-Balart, Mario, 78
Displaced Persons Act of 1948, 39
See also refugees
Dominican Republic, **17**
D'Rivera, Paquito, 85
dual immersion. *See* education

education, 89–91
See also language
employment, 16, 73–75
Enhanced Border Security and Visa Entry Reform Act (2002), 41–42, **43**
Estefan, Gloria, 85, 102
Ethiopia, 31
ethnicity, 18, 21, 37, 40, 45
exiles (Cuban), 16, 18–19, 49–50, 53, 71–72, 76, 97
  Freedom Flights, 54, 57–58, 60
  Golden Exiles, 53, 55–56, 57–58, 59
  See also Cuban Americans; refugees

Fermi, Laura, 39
Festival de la Calle Ocho (Eighth Street Festival), 82–83
See also holidays
Florida, 15, 48–51, 61, 62, 66, 99
Freedom Flights, 54, 57–58, 60
See also exiles (Cuban)

de Gálvez, Bernardo, 48
García, Andy, 102
García Menocal, Mario, 52
Goizueta, Roberto, 102
Golden Exiles, 53, 55–56, 57–58, 59
See also exiles (Cuban)
Gomez, Max, **71**
González, Elián, 92–95, 99
González, Elisabet, 93
González, Juan Miguel, 93–95
Gore, Al, 98
Grant, Madison, 38
Grant, Ulysses S., 50
Grau san Martín, Carlos Ramón, 24
Grito de Baire (Cry of Baire), **82**, 83
See also holidays
Grito de Yara (Cry of Yara), **82**, 83
See also holidays
Guantánamo Bay, Cuba, **15**, 24, 65–66, 67
Guevara, Ernesto "Che," 25, **26**
Guilló, Nemesio and Ernesto, 86

El Habanero, 53
Haiti, **17**, 59–60, 92
Havana, Cuba, 23, 26, 28, 32, 48, 56, 64
Hernández, Liván, 86
Hernández, Orlando, 86
Hijuelos, Oscar, 102
Hispanics. *See* ethnicity
holidays, **81**, 82–84, 86, 87
See also culture
Homeland Security Act of 2002, 42
human rights, 27, 28–29, 30, 31, 32, **34**, 35
Human Rights Watch, 35

illegal immigrants. *See* undocumented immigrants
Illegal Immigration Reform and Immigrant Responsibility Act (1996), 41
immigration
  difficulties of, 89–92
  history of, in Canada, 45–47
  history of, in the United States, 37–45, 59
  rates of, in Canada, **99**

rates of, in the United States, **17**, **33**, 37, 39, 43–44, 56, 57, 60, 61
    reasons for, 21, 31, 32–33, 52, 53, 55–56
    Immigration Act of 1924, 38
        See also quotas
Immigration Act of 1990, 41
Immigration Act of 1952 (Canada), 45–46
Immigration and Nationality Act (1952), 39–40
Immigration and Nationality Act (1965), 40–41
Immigration and Naturalization Service (INS), 41
    See also Department of Homeland Security
Immigration and Refugee Protection Act (Canada), 47
Immigration Reform and Control Act (1986), 41
Industrial and Labor Relations Review, 62–63
Inter-American Commission on Human Rights, 64

Jamaica, **17**
John Paul II (Pope), 34–35, 69
Johnson, Lyndon B., **40**, 58, 91

Kennedy, John F., 28, 29–30, 56, 98

language, 17, 18, 19, 72, 77, 101
    and education, 89–91
Latinos. *See* ethnicity
Laughlin, Harry N., 38
Little Havana, Miami, 73, **78**, 83, **100**
    See also communities
López, Narciso, 50

Maceo, Antonio, 83–84
    See also holidays
Machado, Gerardo, 24, **25**, 52
Manuel de Cagigal, Juan, 48–49
Mariel boatlift, 32–33, 54, 60–64, 77, 90, 91–92
    See also refugees
Marsans, Armando, 86
Martí, José, **22**, 23, 51, **82**, 83
Mas Canosa, Jorge, 78, 102
Mendieta, Carlos, 52
Menéndez, Robert, 78
Miami, Fla., 16, 17–18, 58, 62, 66, 74, 75, 78, 79, 87, 89–90, 93–94, 101

Miguel, Juan. *See* González, Juan Miguel
music, 85
    See also culture

New York City, N.Y., 49–51
Nicaragua, 30–31

Oliva, Tony, 86
Omega 7, 76
"one-and-a-halfers," 76–79
    See also Cuban Americans
Operation Peter Pan, 58
    See also exiles (Cuban)

Palmeiro, Rafael, 86
Pataki, George, **71**
Payá Sardiñas, Oswaldo, 35
Pearson, Lester, 46
Pérez, Atanasio (Tony), 86, 102
Platt Amendment, 23, 24
    See also Cuba; United States
points system, 46–47, 69
    See also Canada
population
    Cuban, in Canada, 15
    Cuban Americans, 15, 47–48, **72**
    Porto, Enrique, 86
    Prío Socarrás, Carlos, 24, 52

quotas, 38, 39–41

"rafter" crisis, 33, 54, 64–67, 92, 101
    See also refugees
Reagan, Ronald, 98
Refugee Act of 1980, 41
    See also refugees
refugees, **15**, 32–33, **37**, 39, 41, 44, 45, 47, 58–59, **68**
    from the Mariel boatlift, 32–33, 54, 60–64, 77, 90, 91–92
    and the "rafter" crisis, 33, 54, 64–67, 92, 101
    See also Cuban Americans; exiles (Cuban)
religion, 84
    See also holidays
Rodríguez, Manuel and Lydia, 75
Ros-Lehtinen, Ileana, 78, 102

Sandanistas, 30–31
    See also communism
Sandoval, Arturo, 85

Schumer, Charles, **71**
Scully, C. D., 38
siesta, 81
    See also culture
Somoza, Anastasio, 30
Soviet Union, 27, 29–30, 32–33, 56, 71
Spain, 21–23, 48–51, 53, 81
St. Augustine, Fla., 48, **49**

Temporary Quota Act of 1921, 38
    See also quotas
Ten Years War, 22, 50, 51, **82**, 83
terrorism, 42–43
Three Kings Day (El Día de los Tres Reyes Magos), **81**, 83
    See also holidays
Tiant, Luis, 86
Torres de Ayala, Laureano, 48
Trinidad and Tobago, **17**

undocumented immigrants, 41, 42, 44
Union City, N.J., 58, 74, 75, 78, 79
    See also communities
United Nations Human Rights Commission, 32, 35
United States
    and Cuba, 21, 23–24, 27–30, 31–34, 48–52, 56, 66–67
    Cuban population in, 15, 47–48, **72**
    immigration history, 37–45, 59
    immigration rates, **17**, **33**, 37, 39, 43–44, 56, 57, 60, 61
USA PATRIOT Act (2002), 41–42, **43**
USS *Maine*, 23

Varela, Félix, 53
La Virgen de la Caridad (Our Lady of Charity), 84
    See also holidays
visas, 38, 41–42, 44
    See also quotas
Vuelos de la Libertad (Freedom Flights), 54, 57–58, 60
    See also exiles (Cuban)

War of Independence (1895), 51, **82**, 83
Washington, George, 48–49
"wet foot/dry foot" policy, 67, **68**, 92
    See also "rafter" crisis
World War I, 38
World War II, 38, 39, 45

Contributors

Senior consulting editor STUART ANDERSON is an adjunct scholar at the Cato Institute and executive director of the National Foundation for American Policy. From August 2001 to January 2003, he served as executive associate commissioner for Policy and Planning and Counselor to the Commissioner at the Immigration and Naturalization Service. He spent four and a half years on Capitol Hill on the Senate Immigration Subcommittee, first for Senator Spencer Abraham and then as Staff Director of the subcommittee for Senator Sam Brownback. Prior to that, Stuart was Director of Trade and Immigration Studies at the Cato Institute, where he produced reports on the military contributions of immigrants and the role of immigrants in high technology. Stuart has published articles in the Wall Street Journal, New York Times, Los Angeles Times, and other publications. He has an M.A. from Georgetown University and a B.A. in Political Science from Drew University. His articles have appeared in such publications as the *Wall Street Journal*, *New York Times*, and *Los Angeles Times*.

MARIAN L. SMITH served as the senior historian of the U.S. Immigration and Naturalization Service (INS) from 1988 to 2003, and is currently the immigration and naturalization historian within the Department of Homeland Security in Washington, D.C. She studies, publishes, and speaks on the history of the immigration agency and is active in the management of official 20th-century immigration records.

PETER HAMMERSCHMIDT is director general of national cyber security at Public Safety Canada. He previously served as First Secretary (Financial and Military Affairs) for the Permanent Mission of Canada to the United Nations. Before taking this position, he was a ministerial speechwriter and policy specialist for the Department of National Defence in Ottawa. Prior to joining the public service, he served as the Publications Director for the Canadian Institute of Strategic Studies in Toronto. He has a B.A. (Honours) in Political Studies from Queen's University, and an MScEcon in Strategic Studies from the University of Wales, Aberystwyth.

PETE SPRANGER is a freelance writer and editor. He lives in Chicago with his wife and two children. This is his first book.

Picture Credits

Page
- 1: Meunierd / Shutterstock.com
- 2: Rob Crandall / Shutterstock.com
- 9: used under license from Shutterstock, Inc.
- 12: Stacey Newman / Shutterstock.com
- 14: U.S. Department of Defense
- 20: Hulton/Archive/Getty Images
- 23: Hulton/Archive/Getty Images
- 25: Bettmann/Corbis
- 26: Hulton/Archive/Getty Images
- 30: Hulton/Archive/Getty Images
- 34: Tim Chapman/Miami Herald/Getty Images
- 38: OTTN Publishing
- 41: OTTN Publishing
- 42: Official White House Photo by Pete Souza
- 44: U.S. Coast Guard
- 47: Hulton/Archive/Getty Images
- 48: OTTN Publishing
- 51: Hulton/Archive/Getty Images
- 58: Tim Chapman/Miami Herald/Getty Images
- 61: Stephen Ferry/Liaison/Getty Images
- 66: Rmnoa357 / Shutterstock.com
- 69: Kamira / Shutterstock.com
- 70: JonathanCollins / Shutterstock.com
- 72: Oneinchpunch / Shutterstock.com
- 73: Msubhadeep / Shutterstock.com
- 75: Rmnoa357 / Shutterstock.com
- 76: Robert Nickelsberg/Liaison/Getty Images
- 78: Mario Tama/Getty Images
- 81: Monika Graff/Getty Images
- 82: Miami2you / Shutterstock.com
- 83: TaYa294 / Shutterstock.com
- 84: Debby Wong / Shutterstock.com
- 86: Kamira / Shutterstock.com
- 88: used under license from Shutterstock, Inc.
- 93: Joe Raedle/Getty Images
- 94: Anthony Correia / Shutterstock.com
- 96: Official White House Photo by Pete Souza
- 100: Crush Rush / Shutterstock.com